TIGHT SPIRAL

TIGHT SPIRAL

Michael J Gill

Copyright © 2014 Michael J Gill

The moral right of the author has been asserted.

Apart from any fair dealing for the purposes of research or private study, or criticism or review, as permitted under the Copyright, Designs and Patents Act 1988, this publication may only be reproduced, stored or transmitted, in any form or by any means, with the prior permission in writing of the publishers, or in the case of reprographic reproduction in accordance with the terms of licences issued by the Copyright Licensing Agency. Enquiries concerning reproduction outside those terms should be sent to the publishers.

Matador
9 Priory Business Park
Kibworth Beauchamp
Leicestershire LE8 0RX, UK
Tel: (+44) 116 279 2299
Fax: (+44) 116 279 2277
Email: books@troubador.co.uk
Web: www.troubador.co.uk/matador

ISBN 978 1783063 000

British Library Cataloguing in Publication Data.
A catalogue record for this book is available from the British Library.

Typeset in Aldine401 BT Roman
Printed and bound in the UK by TJ International, Padstow, Cornwall

Matador is an imprint of Troubador Publishing Ltd

It is not in the stars to hold our destiny
But in ourselves

- William Shakespeare

Part One

Chapter 1

Harry woke suddenly. He glanced at the alarm clock. 5:45AM. His eyes, wide like a cat's at night, fixed intensely on the ceiling. He shivered and wondered why he had not checked the forecast yesterday. Heavy rain in this part of Texas always freaked him out. His only fear in Texas: tornados! The noise on the roof seemed more intense than normal. He quickly dressed and headed through the living room.

"What a noise out there," he said to Tigger, his cat, who was rubbing his legs waiting for her early morning wander. He opened the front door and yelled, "You bastards!" as ice pellets hit his face. He scrambled to retrieve the weekly flyers with more than a few profanities to wake up the neighbors. Back inside, Tigger had decided on an early breakfast.

He sat on the sofa, coffee in hand. He couldn't remember the last time he was up so early in the morning. He would have a coffee, shower and head down for training early – impress the coach. It had been almost two weeks since his last workout. Leading the University of Texas football team to a win at the Cotton Bowl on New Year's Day had been totally incredible. Between the parties and TV interviews, he had not a minute to himself. He was the first British quarterback ever to play in the USA, never mind winning a bowl championship.

He thought about Austin, Texas, and how he'd made the right choice moving here. It was his granddad's idea. G Pops, as he called him, lived here and had been his inspiration. He loved the heat, the people, and only wished to God it was not tornado alley. Would a twister follow the ice pellets? He shivered at the thought.

Harry sipped on his coffee, wondering if there was anything more evil on this planet than a tornado. His mum always said thunder was god being angry with all of us and he assumed therefore that a tornado was a message that he was really pissed off!

They trick you, hiding in the sky with mustard and green colors, not always high winds like a hurricane. Often quiet, and then boom! Destruction in the blink of the eye!

A hurricane is devastating but you see it in advance. The huge covering of red and green on the TV station's Doppler or your website weather map. Twisters are unpredictable little bastards with minds of their own. They have no rhyme or reason. Meteorologists cannot and never will determine their path of destruction.

He pictured the last one to hit near Austin, just a few miles north. He imagined the long arm appearing out of a dense cloud; *I will have some of that,* it seemed to roar. A village, trailer park, cows – lifted up in a second and consumed in the violent twisting column of immeasurable power. Eaten up and discarded many miles away.

"Okay enough about tornadoes. Think positive," he muttered and headed for the shower.

Thirty minutes later, the parking lot outside his apartment was like an ice rink. The ice pellets had stopped and left a gleaming white carpet as far as the eye could see. He started up the pickup truck and walked around kicking at the ice. *This is going to be fun,* he thought sarcastically while admiring his truck.

First thing he bought with the help of G Pops was a good strong pickup. It was a Dodge which seemed to suit his style. Not too flash, but reliable – gets any job done. When in Rome, he had thought when moving to Texas. Get a truck, hat, and boots, and a gorgeous Texan girl. He found all of them and was over the moon with life.

I'll have to be careful, he thought when climbing back into the cab. These things are great, except light on the back end. *Don't brake hard and I will be all right. Let's do this,* he thought.

He managed literally to skate out of the parking lot and down towards I 35. He entered the ramp and was 5 miles from the gym. He wished he had not taken the highway. Cars and trucks were scattered on both sides of the road. He stared in amazement at the fenders hanging off vehicles, radiators steaming from cars plowing into the barrier. There were so many vehicles sliding out of control.

He heard a noise to his left, like a grating sound, coming nearer, louder. He took a quick glance. An 18-wheeler out of control, coming, coming at him, on him…

Chapter 2

Meanwhile, Harry's Granddad, Paul, turned on the news like he did most mornings. The news team was discussing the freak ice storm with Cindy, the meteorologist. Jack, the news anchorman, adjusted his ear piece. His eyes widened, interrupting Cindy and her weather charts.

"We are going live to I 35 with some shocking news. Laine, can you hear us?"

"Yes, Jack!" A reporter yelled over the wind and ice pellet noise. "Our very own UT quarterback Harry Smith, affectionately known as Prince Harry, is in critical condition after being involved in an accident involving several vehicles. At this time the information is sketchy and we will have more news in the next thirty minutes." The camera scanned the highway showing many vehicles overturned, people walking around in a daze and paramedics caring for the wounded.

Paul gazed at the TV screen, his mind blank, his body completely numb. His hands began to shake while coffee spilled on his lap. He would normally shout for his wife, Deborah, in any crisis but she was already up, standing behind him.

"What happened? Talk to me."

"Harry's been in an accident. They said critical condition. Our grandson!" He started moving.

Paul was still in a daze, changing into winter clothes and boots. Fortunately for him, his wife was brilliant in a crisis with her calm Canadian demeanor.

"Do you want me to call James?"

"Not yet," he said, heading for the door. "I'll call him on my mobile. Just let me find out Harry's condition before I call him." He dreaded the thought of telling his son.

She nodded. "Be extra careful on the highway, I know you're good but watch out for all the other maniacs. They're not used to these conditions."

The parking lot was like an ice rink and it took too much time to make the 100 yards to the main complex gate. He made the drive to the hospital, which took about double the normal 15 minutes and ran through the hospital entrance.

A kind nurse with a big smile asked in a Texas drawl, "Who are you here to see?"

"Harry Smith", he stammered. "He's my grandson."

"Oh my God! The UT quarterback? He's in emergency. Let me take you to the waiting area." She took his hand. Texans were so friendly and she certainly had calmed him down. Well, just a tad.

After a while, a nurse appeared and informed him it would still be some hours. He needed some air, have a cig, so he went outside. He knew smoking was dumb and had tried several times to quit. A crisis only magnified the urge. He lit one up, took a long pull and remembered his own accident.

He'd been only 17-years-old, his whole life ahead of him. The only part he could ever remember in the middle of the terror was his body shaking from head to foot, lying down in a huge dyke full of water. Then a friendly lady was telling him the ambulance was on its way and was there anything else she could do for him?

"Light me a cigarette and hold it in my mouth," he had asked while his body was trembling from head to toe. She found them in his pocket and stayed with him there until after he had blacked out. He'd found out later how close he'd been to losing all of his right leg in that accident. The surgeon and his team had prepared for an amputation, only to find he had lost too much blood. Twenty-three operations, two years of his life lying in a hospital bed, the leg was saved. Score one up to social medicine, and the doctors and nurses in the UK for that small miracle.

"Fuck! Harry without a leg, or two years in hospital," he snapped out loud. He broke down and cried, sobbed like a baby and walked with no purpose around the hospital grounds. He came to the main entrance and crowds were assembling. There were so many cars, vans, flashing lights of cameras, cell phones and iPods.

Two young girls stood crying, holding a placard that said in big letters, "Prince Harry we love you!" It suddenly dawned on him: the impact of the accident on the university, the city of Austin. The game of football was so big here.

He remembered the first game he attended: the UT Longhorns at home to Texas AM with 82,000 fans. And that was just a regular season game. The noise, the bands – it was electric. Years later, how could he have dreamed his grandson would be the starting QB for one of the top universities in the USA. *Was* the starting QB. That was all up in the air now.

"Are you okay sir?" asked one of the girls with the placard.

"Yes," he choked, pausing to gain composure. "Harry is my grandson."

She yelled to the crowd, "Hey, this is Harry's grandpa!"

Within seconds, a hundred or so students, fans and reporters had circled around him. "What can you tell us about Harry's condition?" A reporter thrust a microphone in his face.

"Look guys, he will be in surgery for quite some time. I know nothing just yet. I will come out on the hour and bring you updates I promise." He held up his hands to ward off any more questions, then walked back in the hospital and into the empty elevator.

Once the door shut he screamed so loud. He looked up at the ceiling. "If you let anything happen to him, I fucking swear this will be it: no more believing in you."

The waiting area was quiet. The operating room door was closed tight. He paced, decided it was time.

He called James in England, told him the news. After a few seconds of uncomfortable silence, he shouted to his wife, Angie, to pick up the other phone.

"Tell me that again, Dad. Slowly this time."

Paul repeated the story. Then he had to move the phone away from his ear through a tirade of screaming.

All he caught was, "It's all your fault with your fucking dreams of Harry living in Texas!"

"When are you coming?" Paul asked, ignoring all the profanities.

Angie's voice came on the phone, quieter, her voice shaking. "Next plane out, of course, as soon as we have all the kids organized with sitters. Probably tomorrow. Call us anytime with updates. And Paul, never mind James. He'll come around."

The next few hours were unbearable. He replayed the phone call over and over in his mind, and his eldest son screaming. He would not feel guilty. Texas was the best for a teenager. The first British quarterback in college football. *No fucking way is anybody to blame.*

Finally, a surgeon appeared. "Are you family?" he asked.

"Yes. I'm his granddad. His mum and dad are on the next plane from England."

"I'm afraid it's not good. He's in a coma."

"What's affected?"

"His brain. Actually the rest of his body is fine – some heavy bruising, but otherwise fine. The severe head trauma is our concern and it will just be a matter of waiting, monitoring and hoping he awakes."

"What can I do, doctor? Please. There must be something."

"The nurse can help you with an information package on coma patients." With that he turned and headed back to the surgery room.

He thought about his time in hospital years ago. He'd wakened from a 48-hour coma alone in a ward with other critical patients. Back in 1970, nobody had a clue. He had played music on a small battery operated radio. One young lad woke up and sang along to a Beatles song. He was diagnosed days later with permanent brain damage. He shuddered.

We will talk to him constantly. His girlfriend Kelly will help, and his mum and dad will be here soon. I'll talk football – lots of it – until he's sick of hearing me and wakes up.

"Damn it!" he shouted.

Chapter 3

Harry was at peace, totally relaxed without a care in the world. The surroundings were odd and yet felt right.

He sat in a leather armchair, feet up in what looked like a sunroom. He looked to his right, which revealed a big window. The view always seemed to be of a sunny day: birds on the feeders, trees and flowers in abundance. Straight ahead was a short and narrow corridor. It was bright and shiny. At the end was a small room. Monitors produced a rhythmic sound. He could only see a portion of the room: the door, an area with a TV, and what looked like the end of a bed with a pair of feet.

He had overheard every conversation from that room for what seemed like eternity. Hours, days – he had no idea. They were talking about him, to him.

"But guys, I'm down here in my sunroom," he would try to say.

His family had been there whenever he looked down the corridor: Mum and Dad nattering on about him coming home to England, Granddad constantly reporting on football games, his girlfriend Kelly crying. He knew them all, loved them to death. And yet, in this place, listening, watching them down the corridor, he was happy. He felt warm and comfortable. But today, for the first time, he felt slightly different.

The door opened in the room, down the corridor. The lovely nurse entered. She checked the two monitors and leaned over the bed and went out of Harry's view. Suddenly, he felt a wet, warm soft material brushing gently over all of his face. It felt good, his skin tingling. His whole body felt different, energized.

She said, "Harry, all of Austin is praying for you. Please wake up. I know how much you like your bed bath." So that was it. He had felt it and it was so good.

"I'm down here," he tried to shout and yet it was a whisper. "I am awake down here. Look down the corridor; I'm the one waving."

The nurse bumped into Kelly at the door, where they exchanged pleasantries and Harry hoped she would not start crying again. He watched her move out of his field of vision next to the bed. He was immediately overcome with the most amazing feeling he had ever experienced. His penis grew to the hardest he could ever recall. First the warm facecloth and now this! He was thinking of making love to Kelly. Kelly was so beautiful. She had the most amazing big brown eyes, a cute tiny nose and that voice. He remembered the first time he heard her speak at the coffee shop on campus. She had a soft Texas drawl with a funny whistle that gently came through her teeth when pronouncing certain words. Her eyes, her voice, made him feel like jelly.

He started to float away, out of the sunroom in the opposite direction from the corridor. Shiny white lights grew brighter with voices in a whisper echoing all around him. He tried hard to listen but could not understand them. In less time than the blink of an eye, he was spinning into space.

The stars were so bright in all directions, some brighter than others. Purples, violets and blues were dancing, while stars, old and shiny new, were packed tightly in spiral arm formations. He had come to a standstill floating in space: a ride on the Milky Way. He looked in the distance, far beyond the amazing spectacle. It was sheer black without a single star. It seemed to be beckoning him.

He closed his eyes, refusing to look in its direction. The pull toward it grew stronger.

Chapter 4

Across the pond in Leeds, Amy Carrington had just about had enough. She read her next assignment – Barnsley at home to Scunthorpe. She would not relish sitting at Oakwell on a frigidly cold winter day.

"No way. That's all I need this weekend," she said loudly at her Mac computer.

"What's up, AC?" shouted one of her male co-workers. Amy turned, gave a serious look in the general direction of the laughing guys and went back to her screen. AC was her nickname in the office, given to her by the lads. And it wasn't just for her initials. Cold as Air Conditioning.

Far from insulted, she was quite happy with their assumption. Outside the office she was always so much happier. Having lunch and a glass of fine wine or champagne would be more her style. She lived for the weekends when she could get out of this boys' club. This Friday night was supposed to be a "girls" night at a new nightclub in the city. Now Barnsley!

Just what I need: sitting in the frigid cold of winter with a wicked hangover reporting on an insignificant football game. She had already bought a new outfit for Friday night and imagined how she would turn a few heads. Amy knew she was a bit of a stunner and liked to hide the fact at work. She was 5ft 5 with long dark hair and big brown eyes. Her naturally tanned complexion looked like she had just been on holiday in the Med. She kept her hair up at work, wearing flat shoes and a Yorkshire flat cap when outside on work assignments. At night, she would let her hair down and wear heels. She always thought tall women had something extra, an air of power about them.

She had dreams of covering fashion and the arts, and her hometown of Leeds had plenty of that to offer. She loved her city and to hell with the job offers she had received from London. She would make it with the only true newspaper in Yorkshire and win the young journalist of the year award. The only position available when she graduated from university last year was an assistant to the sports writer and that meant Barnsley, Huddersfield or even Farsley. "Farsley, boss," she remembered saying.

She put on her coat and headed out of the office. There must be some excuse for a nice lunch at a trendy restaurant. Maybe she would find a Barnsley player to interview and write off her expenses.

"Have a nice day, arseholes," she said to the guys.

"Not so fast, Amy!" shouted her boss.

Shit. What have I done now? She sighed.

"In my office, right this minute." The guys were all smiling, whispering as she went by.

Amy sat, displaying her regular look to the boss: a smile, not too much but enough to remind him she was confident, attractive and an asset to the paper. No doubt she was in trouble, probably over her expenses being too high, again. Her boss peered over his glasses.

"How are you enjoying your first twelve months at the paper?"

"It's fine, boss. I mean, it's not what I was hoping for but the *Yorkshire Gazette* is everything to me."

"Amy, do you remember when I hired you how you said you'd work anything I assigned you except obits?"

She nodded.

"Well, I didn't put you in the life and arts section. I didn't put you in the city news section. I put you in a perfectly wonderful sports department."

"And I'm grateful for the chance ..."

"Your expenses are not acceptable and this will have to be your final warning to bring them in line. You can't have a fancy lunch with wine on a regular basis and expect us to believe you were following a story on a Barnsley or Bradford City player!"

Amy was instantly on the defensive. "What about the story I brought you on the player – you know – the captain of one of our top clubs. I revealed to you he was cross-dresser and that is down to me being in the restaurant at that time."

"Lovely and why did that not make the paper? I will tell you, Amy. You are here to report on football games, not which player is shagging who, etc. etc. Do I make myself clear?

"Yes, boss," she said with a cheesy smile.

"Last warning!" He stabbed a finger in the air to emphasize and shooed her out of his office.

Thank God it was the last Thursday of the month. Tonight was wine night with her dad. She would pop in to her favorite wine shop in the city, slip the bottle in a brown bag and have him guess the wine. Her Dad started brown bag wine parties many years ago when his best mate had organized one at his house. His mate was in the wine business and this apparently was fun.

When she turned sixteen, they had let her participate with a teeny amount in her glass. There were 8 wines at the parties and she got a wicked buzz on. It turned her into a wine nut and she now followed the Gazette wine writer each week and attended one of her classes. Mum would be at yoga classes, but she always left dinner ready in the oven. She had sent a text to her mum earlier today and said the wine would be Italian and begged for lasagna.

After work, she popped in the back door with wine in hand. "Dad? It's me," she shouted over the noise from the TV in the living room.

"In here, love," her dad replied loudly. Odd, he was always in the kitchen on wine night, fussing over the food and the right wine glasses. She wandered into the living room, grabbed the remote and turned the sound down.

"Dad? It's wine night and I have a good one. Where are the glasses?" she asked, puzzled.

"Yes, of course. Wine night." He gave her a hug. "I was flicking channels when I came on last year's Super Bowl on Sky sports. I can't stop watching it. Quite fascinating really."

Amy hit pause on the remote. "Wine time, Dad, and Mum left us lasagna. I'll watch the game with you later." Amy got two glasses and a corkscrew and removed the cork like a true pro. She had learned that at the wine class.

Her dad nosed the wine while Amy made sure the brown bag was covering the bottle. "Italy, I think," he said with a smile.

"Really, Sherlock? Mum made lasagna. Now stop slacking and tell me the region."

"It would be Veneto. No doubt in my mind." He swished the glass for a few seconds, taking a big sip, followed by a chewing motion, finally smacking his lips. "Okay, a Valpolicella, but not plonk, mind. A good one, and if you want more info, I need some lasagna. This is a food wine!"

Amy sipped on her wine, which was just as delicious as she'd thought, with a bite of Mum's amazing lasagna. Cottage cheese and spicy sausage – it was totally loaded. "So tell me more about the wine."

"It's a Superiore from a good producer with excellent structure and perfect balance. Was it expensive?" he asked.

"No. Under ten quid."

"Then at that price, we have a winner this evening: I have no idea which winery produces such a good value Valpol. Please reveal the wine."

She pulled off the brown bag, showing him the label. "Ta-da! Zenato Valpolicella Superiore from the Veneto region. Apparently the shop said it's a family-owned winery on Lake Garda."

"Interesting. I'll check the winery out on the Internet later tonight." Her dad grabbed the remote and turned the TV back on.

She watched the game in sullen silence with her dad for half an hour and finally said, "Sod this, Dad! I look forward to our wine nights all week. Would you please turn the bloody thing off?"

He did and had a look on his face that reminded her of a bloodhound in those Deep South films she would watch on a Sunday afternoon after a roast lunch at the pub.

"You're weird tonight, Dad. Is everything okay?"

"Yes." He laughed. "Of course. I just got so into this American football game. It's fascinating."

"Why hasn't this game taken off in the UK?"

"It will, love. The annual Wembley game featuring two NFL teams now draws in over 80,000 fans."

Amy tidied up the dishes, put on her coat, and went to give her dad a hug. "Turn your game back on," she said, squeezing his arm.

Heading to her car, a thought did occur. American football was far more exciting than the bloody football matches she had to watch and write about week in, week out.

Chapter 5

Ben Shannon sat in his leather swivel chair. His long legs with their alligator skin cowboy boots stretched out over the shiny mahogany desk. The office of his successful finance company offered breathtaking views of Houston, the fourth largest city in the USA.

The clouds were starting to move in and the regular downpour of rain was imminent. Most afternoons the city would experience a thirty-minute shower, often with the intensity of a monsoon. The sun would reappear and steam would rise from the roads and pavements with the temperature never changing from 100 degrees.

He was waiting for a call from the London office – from Andy, his right hand man in Europe. The latest project motivated him: it was something close to his heart.

"I failed once with my ultimate goal, but damned if ever in my life I plan to fail a second time," he said out loud.

He sat back and recalled this time last year and the rocky road to achieving his goal. He had made a decision, a gutsy one, if he said so himself. One of the richest men in the world and yet he could not buy an NFL franchise. He could buy politicians, favors from some of the most influential people in America, but not the one thing he really wanted.

He thought it would be a slam-dunk. The NFL had become the most successful sport in the world, the most profitable and, more importantly, the fairest. The salary cap and draft had worked like charm and now any team had a chance with the Patriots winning last year as complete underdogs. This year he hoped it would be the Houston Texans!

But the NFL had stonewalled him. *Fuck all of them*. He had finally admitted defeat and moved to Plan B. Leeds in Yorkshire, England, would be the target and his grander plan would finally start to unfold.

He recalled that first phone call to London. "I've given up on pursuing an NFL franchise. No-can-fucking-do is all I hear! Here's the deal: I want to get into the BFL and it has to be Leeds. Can you hire a research team and get back to me with scenarios?"

"Boss, I like a fucking challenge but this beats the biscuit!" Andy had said.

"It's cookies, son, not biscuits, and make it happen," he said with a mix of a Yorkshire accent and Texas drawl. "I want the best stadium in England. It will be a full dome without even an option to open the roof. It always fucking rains in England and I want our show to be perfect each home game. This will be like the theatre presenting an epic and nobody gets cold or wet."

He remembered the nineties with the Houston Oilers in the astrodome where everything was perfect. The temperature set at a constant 68. "Yes, a dome, and in the off season we will have events: rock concerts, other sports, you name it. And one other important task, Andy: buy the Leeds Cougars name and any legal holdings. Call me later with some good news."

American football was popular in England these days. Ben had started paying attention a few years ago. When Jacksonville announced they would play a home game in London each season, for the next three years, it was a big deal and gained them many fans out of loyalty and respect. Knowledgeable fans realized they were giving up home field advantage for the Wembley game and that said something to their commitment.

Ben had also paid close attention to the city of Leeds. Hell, he was from there and proud of it. Well, not entirely. Unfortunately, since leaving at 19, he had only been back on the odd occasion – weddings, funerals. He had been too busy building his empire. He preferred the Texas way of life and most of all, Texans. Pitch an idea to a Brit and you get, "Why?" A Texan: "Why not?"

Yorkshire people are the salt of the earth, but they are so pessimistic. In Texas you always try to get a positive out of a negative. Optimism breeds success!

But he was constantly surprised watching the city of Leeds develop in the last ten years. It had become the best city in the North of England. Some had it pegged as better than the capital. Apart from all the tourist attractions, London had become total shit. The capital was full of crime and poverty staring from every angle. Only the tourists seemed oblivious, with their minds set on the tower, the museums, and numerous attractions.

Leeds was always a wealthy city, run by the Jewish community who kept themselves completely under the radar. However, it had taken everybody by surprise to see the modern development, low crime, people smiling with a positive attitude on life. He had looked at the Leeds Cougars' history and they'd had a great team in the eighties. Coincidentally, they had chosen the Cougars for their team name, giving them an unofficial alliance with the University of Houston, his team. He recalled reading the occasional article in the university newsletter on the Cougars football team in England. Unfortunately, the team went into a decline and finished their last season with 10 losses, no wins. That would all change with a hand-picked team and facilities to match the new super-city of Leeds.

Ben liked himself rather a lot; he had done well and enjoyed life to the fullest. To most he was somewhat of an enigma, to the ladies a huge catch – if only he would return their calls. He was tall, handsome, with impeccable fashion sense. What really stood out was his unique accent. He was often mistaken for an Aussie which, while being somewhat of an insult, he used to his advantage. The mix of Yorkshire and Texas had done this and his phrases could be British or Texan as he deemed fit for the circumstances.

Not that his family was originally British. They were originally from Kiev, Ukraine. Polish-Russian Jews. Part of his family went to Galveston and changed their name from Shanas to Shannon, after his great-granddad had read something when they arrived in 1882 about Scots pioneering the South in Louisiana and Texas. They had decided on a new life and a new name, and a good Celtic name made sense. The rest followed suit. It was just easier.

His branch of the family went to Leeds. He was born in Leeds in 1970 and had been one of the lucky ones. Only a small minority could say that back then. The city was known for being violent and depressing in those days. He played, from a small age, for the Moor Allerton golf club in Leeds. The club had the distinction of being the first golf club in Europe to allow Jewish membership in 1929. By the time he tuned 14, his handicap was so low he was beating most of the adult members!

He worked his ass off at school to get a scholarship to the University of Houston. They had the academics and the golf, and was only an hour's drive to family in Galveston. His golf idol was Nick Faldo who also went there, although he had no desire to make pro. Too boring with all that practice time and no guarantee he could make a shit-pile of money.

A business and finance degree was his ultimate goal. Investments made the world tick and he was already pretty good at it. His uncle would show him the stocks in both the UK and the American Dow Jones and he had been a good teacher. He dabbled in penny stocks as a teenager and made some great profit. His uncle would say it's all about research and good timing.

"Speaking of timing, where is Andy with the news, goddamn it," he muttered to himself.

Chapter 6

Harry was back from his latest trip to the stars, sitting back in his armchair in the sunroom. The door to the room down the corridor opened for the third time today and in barged his granddad. G Pops was pacing around the room like his days of coaching football. He took out what looked like a scrap book and began to read. Harry was more interested today and listened with keen attention.

1979 Cotton Bowl, Notre Dame vs. U. of Houston – The Chicken Soup Game. The city of Dallas was encased in ice, as players prepared for the game. Notre Dame QB Joe Montana recalled how the glazed metropolis appeared as he awoke that day. "It was beautiful – beautiful if you were spending the day looking out a window."

But Montana, despite suffering from the flu, could do nothing of the sort, and he boldly took the Irish to a 12-0 first-quarter lead. Houston used its second-quarter wind advantage (in addition to the cold and ice, there was an 18-30 mph wind) to pile up 20 unanswered points. In the third quarter Houston added another 14, as Montana stayed in the locker room, struggling to stay warm. With the score 34-12, there seemed no reason for him to go back outside. "We knew for a fact people were clicking off their TVs all over the country," Notre Dame center Dave Huffman recalled. "You could hear the ratings drop every time Houston went up another point."

But Montana did go back outside, and here the Montana legend began. Not much happened until Notre Dame's Steve Cichy grabbed a Cougar punt blocked by Tom Belden and scampered 33 yards for a TD. Montana connected with Vagas Ferguson on a two-point conversion to bring the Irish within two TDs with 7:25 left. On their next possession, Notre Dame drove 61 yards with Montana running the last three into the end zone, then threw for another successful two-point conversion with 4:15 remaining. 34-28. There it remained, until the Irish got the ball for a final chance. With the clock reading :00, Montana connected with Kris Haines on an 8-yard TD pass, and walk-on kicker Joe Unis nailed the PAT. Notre Dame 35, Houston 34.

What revived the sick and cold Notre Dame QB? Chicken soup. "It was a magical combo – an Italian leading the Irish to triumph thanks to a traditional Jewish remedy." Paul placed the newspaper clipping down on the bed and breathed in deep.

"Harry, you know Joe was a better quarterback than that nancy-looking California boy! Tom Brady is not a patch on Joe Montana," shouted his Granddad.

Harry had just about had enough of Joe Montana. He knew that Brady had all the records except one. 4-0 in Super Bowl wins. Brady had just won another Super Bowl to make his record 4-2.

His brain had been quiet up until that point. Totally relaxed and enjoying the peace and quiet in his sunroom. However, something inside him was changing. He was feeling wonderful sensations for the first time today and now his head felt like it would explode. His brain was running stats of Brady and Montana. Out of all the QB's in history, Tom was the best. His body lifted gently off the chair. He was floating down the corridor, stats still rolling through his mind. Down the corridor for the first time!

★ ★ ★

Paul paced around the hospital room mumbling "my fault" repeatedly. He stopped at the window. A rain storm was brewing. A strange feeling came over him – paranoia – yet he couldn't see a soul. The hair on his neck tingled. He turned to look at the bed.

Harry was awake and smiling. "Hey, G Pops," he said. "Tom Brady is the best quarterback ever to play the game. Never mind Montana."

Chapter 7

The phone rang and Ben sat up quickly, flicked on the phone monitor with Andy in view on the 70-inch screen.

"Hey boss, don't tell me you have me on that screen. I hate them; make me look like a proper wanker."

"Give me good news or you will have much harsher words describing you than wanker."

"Boss, we won't be starting next season for more than one reason. The BFL won't expand the league." He paused, waiting for Ben. Getting no answer, he continued. "We have found one piece of land that will work."

"Finally some good news," Ben sighed.

"Sorry. It does have problems. The data should be in your folder."

Ben brought up the file on the second screen. He paused and began to read the story from Andy on his second monitor.

"Pudsey? You prick!" he yelled. "I am not having a team called Pudsey! Sounds like a children's book. And besides – my roots are Leeds – mighty Leeds!" Loides: the Kingdom of Leeds, he recollected from local history at school. "Yes we will have the modern version of that kingdom and our team will be the Leeds Cougars. Goddamn it!" he bellowed.

Andy stammered, "No, boss! I have all the papers being

couriered overnight on the Leeds Cougars. You will own the name by tomorrow. This is just the land."

He went back to the monitor and read the story. It became quite intriguing.

"Andy, I have a few initial questions for you, and I will absorb this and get back to you. Refresh my memory. Is Pudsey under Leeds or Bradford?"

"Leeds. Has been since the eighties."

"Well that is a good start."

Andy interrupted. "But – and this is a big but – the land is owned by both cities. A joint venture."

"Goddamn! Bradford being involved is not good. These two never did anything together. So it's right in the middle, about 4 miles between each city, correct?"

"Yes, boss, and it's growing. The latest population figures are close to 50,000."

His mind kicked into another gear. "So we've got a potential captive audience if we can make Bradford happy. What would be the total population of the two cities and surrounding area?"

"Well, Bradford is one third of over a million, collectively with Leeds. In the West Yorkshire area we would attract over 3 million."

"Liking it so far," said Ben with a tad more enthusiasm than a few minutes ago. "The scam on this piece of land had been handled all wrong. Most British councils are just not savvy in business. The government is no better. I will get up to speed with this."

"Boss, what about the expansion problem? We don't have a current team."

"We will Andy. Trust me."

"When is the BFL committee meeting next?"

"I thought you might ask: two weeks from today."

"Right. We'll make a surprise visit. Get me a meeting set up for the day after with Bradford."

"You're flying over, boss?"

"You bet!"

He pushed back his chair and put his legs up on the desk, his shiny cowboy boots now crossed over each other.

This is no different to Minneapolis & Saint Paul's, the twin cities, he considered. *They both share the Vikings and they are based in Minneapolis. They are about the same distance away from each other. This site would be perfect. I just don't want to deal with Bradford. I'll have to come up with a sweet deal to make them happy. The expansion problem was much easier than this problem.*

The BFL consisted of eight teams owned by large corporations. They had bought into the notion that the NFL would eventually set up a farm team system whereby each team would be an expansion franchise owned by each NFL team. A special extended college draft system would be implemented.

Some NFL owners had even considered moving their team to the UK. The only problem with that scenario was it would have to be London and the Ravens owner would have none of that!

The latest news Ben had from his inside sources was that within the next two years the NFL would make a move – regardless of any obstacles, there would be one or a full league of NFL expansion teams in the UK.

He had also received a full report on the only Yorkshire

team in the league. Sheffield was owned by a company that had invested heavily in mining. They were sure the government in question was totally behind their venture until the leadership changed last week. Officials announced yesterday the deal was off and their stock was plummeting. He had made a call to his top financial advisor with instructions to buy Sheffield lock, stock and barrel. *I will get into the NFL through the back door,* he had decided.

Poor Andy would read about this in the morning paper. Always good to keep your people on their toes, let them know the boss will always come through.

He sat further back in his chair, his head spinning. He had kept himself so busy with work for these past twenty years that he rarely thought about home. The UK was home: he understood this fact. Brits leave in their thousands each year, searching for the land of milk and honey with lots of sunshine. But trying to take England out of an Englishman is just not possible.

While you're sitting in the lap of luxury with sunshine and your Corona, London is hosting the Olympics. Each and every one of those Brits, Ben included, were so proud, it took all their willpower not to pack it all in and be on the next flight back.

England was the best country in the world – of that he had no doubt. A place to make a shit pile of money with good weather, it was not. Speaking of travel and planes … *Wait a minute Ben, you are a fucking genius. Bradford will be just fine.*

"The Cougar Dome will be built. I know it!" he said aloud.

Chapter 8

"Look at that pass from Brady! No way could Montana have thrown that ball, even if Rice was wide open," Harry said with a chuckle.

He had his Dad and G Pops at the flat watching the game. "Another beer, guys?" They both nodded while Harry headed for the fridge. He would have to stick with Coke or, better still, OJ.

He felt good, the best in days. His only wish being a beer or five. *No way man, on these drugs!* His prescription still had 10 more days to complete.

He sat back down to the game when a knock sounded on the door. "That's funny," he said to his Dad and G Pops. "No way does anybody knock on a door in Texas. You call first. We all know that." There are signs everywhere in all apartment complexes reading, "no solicitors". That had made him laugh when he first got here. No attorneys knocking on your door was fine with him.

He opened the door to see Kelly with a big smile on her face, wearing a tank top and shorts.

"What are you doing cooped inside on a day like this?"

Harry invited her in. G Pops and Dad greeted her and made a spot on the couch while Harry got her a cold beer.

"So what have you been up to? What was the verdict from the doc?"

"I have to rest for six to nine months. I have bruising on my brain," he said in a zombie-like voice. "I can study if I feel my head is up to the task. No chance of doing sports, heavy drinking, late nights. I'm going to be a barrel of laughs."

"Shit, that's awful. Hey do you feel like a drive out to our favorite spot? We don't need to drink. I'll drive."

"Slowly please?"

"Okay, sweetie." She giggled.

"Harry, I realize you need a break but we did tell the doctor we would be here for you 24/7," said his dad while Paul nodded in agreement.

"I'll be back in a few hours, ready for the evening game. You have my word."

"No calling in a bar on the way back?"

Harry hesitated at the door. "Don't worry, you two. I'll be fine."

Their favorite spot was a quiet bay on a large lake just north of Austin. Harry sat on the rocky beach listening to the gentle ripples dancing on the granite rocks while Kelly was hugging his waist. This was a good idea; *I needed fresh air, the open space.* He squeezed her back tightly, feeling at peace with himself, no thoughts of the past or the future, just now, in this moment.

He was lost in thought until Kelly shifted her arm. She moved a few feet from him. Harry took in the view, realizing one of his attractions to her was a great body. She was so fit, with shapely legs, her shoulders with just the right amount of muscle, her chest proudly revealing her firm 36 C breasts. *Wow!* She took off her top followed by her shorts and panties.

"Let's go skinny dipping," she yelled while running into the water.

Harry followed her into the warm water, his whole body relaxing. He had not been in the water since the accident and now remembered how much he loved coming here.

After a long swim, he glided in close to her instinctively. His favorite way to make love was in the water; her amazing legs wrapped around his waist. The water was so relaxing – the rhythmic current of the lake, a soft breeze, just the right amount of buoyancy to tread water with ease.

She wrapped her legs around him, kissing him hard, her tongue darting, probing inside his mouth. He felt nothing! She took hold of him like always to guide him inside her.

"Hey, the water is warm not cold." She giggled nervously. "What's happening down there?"

Harry was embarrassed. He had no idea what was going on. "No idea, babe. I think it's time we got out." He swam back to shore feeling totally pissed off. *Can't drink, can't shag – what the fuck can I do?*

She came out and wrapped a big blanket around the two of them, stroking his hair. "It will just be a post reaction to the accident, no worries. If it happens again we can always get you on a dose of Viagra." They both laughed. Harry's laugh was, however, a compete façade. He was totally gutted.

They sat quietly looking out to the lake for quite some time. Kelly lit a small joint, sucking in hard.

"Try a bit, sweetie. It might help."

He hesitated. Finally, he succumbed, knowing that familiar feeling. Chilling out after that episode would be a good idea. He drew back the smoke, holding it for a few seconds, slowly letting the smoke glide down into his lungs. His mind became instantly clear, his mood decisive.

"Kelly, I have to tell you something important." He finally broke the silence. "I'm going back to England and probably for good. I don't know what it is but certainly not the silly things I miss like fish and chips and pints of real ale. I have a weird feeling, like a strong pull, some new connection to home."

"Well, I'll have to work things out here and then join you."

He smiled dishonestly.

Kelly is gorgeous, the best girl I've ever had. And yet, for some unknown reason, I don't see her in my future.

Chapter 9

Amy read her email message one more time.

She had interviewed for a writing position with a London fashion magazine last week. This was confirmation she had been successful, beating over 200 applicants apparently. *Nice work, girl!*

It was more writing for their busy blog than outside assignments. However, it was better than reporting on dreary football games.

"Amy! Office, please," she heard from her boss.

The guys were making a chopping motion to their throats.

She stalked into the office, wondering what it could be now. *I cut back my bloody expenses by over 50% last month. Sod it! I will take the new job offer in London*, she immediately decided.

Before she could sit down, her boss was up from his chair.

"Amy, I have a promotion for you. Not a pay increase, until you have proven yourself. However, it's a good assignment and something you can get your teeth into. Right up your alley, really."

It's about time. "The arts? Music? Fashion?" she asked.

Her boss laughed. "Stop being a twit. You are a sports writer. Although for the next year there will be some diversity with this assignment and it will give you time to research the game."

"A year? Boss, give me a break. I had footie games sorted in a week."

"Did you know we are the only English-speaking country in the world that calls soccer football?" he said while looking at Amy over his glasses. "Your new assignment is football. American football."

Amy laughed, which was unusual for her in the workplace.

"When you pull yourself together I will give you the latest scoop. This just came in a few minutes ago: one of the richest men in the world is buying the vacant piece of land in Pudsey. Ben Shannon is a local lad, born right here in bloody Leeds. He is meeting with the Mayor of Bradford in the morning, I just heard from my source. If he can convince Bradford to go with this deal, he will announce his plans for a domed stadium to be built in time for next season.

"He apparently wants the stadium to be the best in Europe. The Leeds Cougars American football team is official and ready to play in the BFL next year, now that Shannon has purchased the team in Sheffield. We'll need someone to cover this, of course.

"Amy Carrington, you will be our Cougar girl," he said with a chuckle.

Her mind was spinning with all the possibilities. She knew absolutely nothing about the game of American football. Why the hell didn't she watch more of that Super Bowl game with her dad? *No worries*, she thought, *Dad loves the game and he will help me.*

If I play my cards right this will lead into covering fashion, entertainment, life and arts. I will wing it on the game; I mean, it can't be any harder to report than our game of football.

Stay cool, she thought. *Make out I am doing him a favor.*

"Well thanks, boss. Fancy all my mates calling me the Cougar girl at 24 years of age! I will do it, but just to show my full commitment to the paper."

"Get to Bradford in the morning and make sure you get a quote from Ben Shannon."

She opened the door to see the office staff scampering back to their desks. They had definitely been listening at the door.

One lad shouted, "American football will be so big! Bigger than Leeds United!"

Duh.

Another shouted, "Hey the new lad in the mail room is 19-years-old. How about you take him out on a date, Cougar girl?"

She smiled, stayed calm and gave them all the finger as she confidently exited the office.

In the car she sent an email to the fashion magazine.

Thank you so much, however, I will have to decline your offer. I am staying with the Yorkshire Gazette, she typed with a nervous feeling in her stomach.

This had better work out, she thought.

Chapter 10

Ben felt comfortable flying around the world. His Gulfstream private jet was equipped with all the comforts of home. This flight was easy compared to Asia and Australia. Eleven hours across the pond was a walk in the park, except he could never sleep for long spells. Cat naps on the hour was the best he could muster.

He sipped a Tattinger champagne while looking at the wine menu. *A Borolo from Piemonte, Northern Italy, with my steak*, he decided. Ben was extremely proud of his wine collection, which was reputed as one of the top fifty in the world based on dollar amount and diversity.

He had become hooked on wine in his student days. He would frequent a huge liquor store right in the center of downtown Houston. Back then, the downtown district had nothing going on. Nightlife and all the great bars were just on the fringe of downtown. The liquor store stood alone in a sleazy area with derelict buildings, under a busy highway bridge. Inside was the Aladdin's cave of wine.

Once he had earned his first million, he began the collection. It was unlike most other wine collections, where the focus was not all on Bordeaux futures. The tag of old world/new world was not important to him. The vintage, the people who made it, their history and tradition was far more important. One of his favorite Argentina Malbec wineries was built and producing wine in 1861. The wine industry called Argentina new world. *Bunch of snobs that are too narrow-minded to know jack shit*, he would often think. His pride and joy was his collection of Italian reds, which was more extensive than any other collector in the world. Borolo, Brunello, and Amarone: he had them all, along with an extensive vintage range of Sassicaia.

He continued to relax, deep in thought of his student days in Houston and how he'd always dreamed of living in River Oaks. He had fallen in love with the area back in '89 when he would be a regular visitor to the arty Montrose area and the new-wave nightclubs. River Oaks was only a mile away in distance but may as well have been a million miles away from the people in Montrose. It would seem like entering an oasis after trekking through a desert mirage to him. It did not seem to belong in this area, and yet that is what made it so appealing. Every home was a million dollars and all around this small area was cheap housing, Goth nightclubs and Mexican restaurants.

River Oaks was built into a perfect square. Wide boulevards adopted the roman grid system. Every house was large and kept impeccable with neat manicured gardens and giant swimming pools secluded in the rear of the property. This was its own community right slap in the middle of the hustle and bustle of a big city. Yet it was tranquil, peaceful, with colonial and Tudor style houses – each was shaded by glorious trees and shrubs, with azaleas in bunches.

One day he would live in this urban paradise, he had thought at the time. Now he did.

His meal and wine was delicious. He had hired a top chef

from Italy and kept fine wines on board the plane. He adjusted the seat to relax and try to sleep. He knew, as always, it would only be catnaps. His eyes were heavy, ready to sleep – for more than thirty minutes, he hoped.

Ben was in deep thought. Not good thoughts. So he turned his attention to a manila folder on his table. His top genie for the company had sent a dossier. The London Ravens owner – Denis Bazan.

Ben had been the first businessman in the world to employ a genie. In fact, the nickname was given to his top genie when Ben's company had been featured in a top business magazine.

His genie was essentially a James Bond type with incredible computer skills. Raymond Bailey was his name. He had been trained in martial arts, worked for a special department for the British government on covert missions that always stayed way under the radar. Raymond was also one of the best computer hackers in the world. He made the Bulgarians look like shit. However, on paper he was only known for his genealogy skills. Raymond had started his genealogy company after retirement, merely looking for a pastime.

Ben had met him at a wine dinner several years ago and they both took a liking to each other. Ben was the wine connoisseur, while Raymond was an aficionado of single malt Scotch whisky.

"Want to do serious business with someone? Check their family tree?" Ben had said after learning of Raymond's pastime. "I would hire you in heartbeat."

He could never read all this on the flight. His eyes were

becoming heavy. He quickly scanned the fifty-page document. Anybody that had crossed Denis Bazan had disappeared. He seemed to be the last Brit with enough power to promote racism, and get away with it. His private henchmen were known for causing havoc, using scare tactics all over the country – the world for that matter. The sex industry and drug trafficking were just a scratch on the surface of Bazan's empire.

He muttered to himself, "Evil son of a bitch."

He tried to forget. He must sleep, have his A game for tomorrow.

The bloody London Ravens kept flashing through his mind. They were unbeaten in all games for the last three seasons. They donned an all-black uniform, had defense like a brick wall, intimidated all opponents. Denis Bazan's fucking team. He would change that.

The Raven is a mystical bird, one of the smartest creatures on the planet. He pictured images of those big black birds he had seen on his many visits to the Tower of London, knee-deep around his legs. Protecting their precious tower. Watching him. If they ever flew away, the British Crown would fall, or so the prophecy said.

Ben tossed and turned – *Ravens. They take your soul to whichever place they decide. Heaven or Hell.*

Chapter 11

Ben and Andy climbed out of the stretch limo. Ben admired the small mews tucked away from the busy area of Kensington. He liked an area just south named the French Quarter where one could enjoy pastries that rivaled any in Paris. The mews was laid out like most in London, with the traditional cobbled street, elegant Victorian houses – all shiny white and clean.

They entered the BFL headquarters reception area, which was the complete opposite of the exterior, with modern décor, shiny glass tables and pictures of the teams. *Way too many of the Ravens*, he thought.

"Good morning," said Andy to the receptionist.

"What can I do for you gents?" she replied in a strong cockney accent.

"We are here to see the committee on an urgent matter."

"You will have to make an appointment," she said firmly.

Ben had already worked out they were meeting upstairs on the second floor and was climbing the stairs two steps at a time with Andy scrambling to catch up.

Ben pushed through the door. Eight elderly gents, seated around a long oak table, looked in astonishment.

He announced, "How are y'all doing, gentlemen?" as he took off his hat. "I am Ben Shannon and I wish to discuss my proposal for a new team."

"Sir," the man at the head of the table said, "you can't just barge in here unannounced. We are in the middle of an important meeting."

"I've just flown in from Texas," declared Ben. "I just have one official announcement and I'll be on my way. I'm now the owner of the Sheffield Stars and the team is moving to Leeds. The new team will be the Leeds Cougars and we will be ready for the season."

"I say, young man," said another guy, "I'm not sure if that is in the rules."

"Yep. It's all fine. I had both my lawyer in Houston and a top solicitor right here in The Smoke check your rules with a fine-tooth comb. Andy, give the kind gentleman here a copy of the papers."

"Gentlemen, thank you for your time. The story should be in the newspapers tonight and we'll send the league our stadium address in due course," explained Andy while Ben had already turned to leave the room.

They left the building and got back into the limo.

"One down, one to go, Andy." He poured himself a scotch. "We paid more than we should for Sheffield but now we will be the only Yorkshire team. I want a PR marketing campaign in place ASAP. Anybody in Yorkshire will receive a discount on tickets to allow for travel. I want all of Yorkshire coming to our games."

"Did you ever consider naming the team Yorkshire Cougars, boss?"

"No way, Jose. Has to be Leeds. We are the capital of the North, done deal. Now let's get ready for Bradford. It will require a sweet deal and I have one in mind."

They discussed his plan on the train from Kings Cross, London to Leeds. They had booked first class, which was almost empty of passengers. Once out of the city traffic, the train whizzed along at great speed and the motion put Ben at ease and in a creative thinking mode.

"It's good, boss. I think it will work." Andy commented while trying to focus on *The Sun* newspaper he was reading, and in particular the page-three girl. Andy continued with a thought completely off subject. He did have a problem staying focused on the odd occasion.

"Boss, why do we travel by train with all the money you have and all?"

"I like the train. Always have since I was a kid. One of my favorite places to visit was always the steam train society in Haworth. I actually donated money to the restoration of one of their locomotives. Great for the kids to ride on those steam trains from the old days. My dad was nuts about them and went trainspotting on his school holidays. Besides, Andy, having money does not mean you have to flaunt it."

Andy nodded gingerly, putting his head deep into his newspaper.

They arrived in Leeds bang on time and Andy had booked a private limousine service. He had sent a text to the company and by the time they walked to the main entrance, the car was there.

"Driver, make sure we go via Pudsey. Do you know the piece of land that has been vacant for years?" asked Andy.

"Too bloody long, excuse my French. Please tell me you are going to buy it."

"Driver, what is your name?" inquired Ben in the back.

"Brian, sir," he replied with a touch of a stutter.

"Brian, we will and, mark my words, the whole of Yorkshire will be happy."

It was a sight for sore eyes when they made a brief stop. So much potential, but right now it was just wasteland sitting there doing nothing.

"This will work. Good find, Andy."

The limo came into the centre of Bradford, passing the famous photography museum and the Alhambra theatre. They arrived at City Hall with a few minutes to spare. A beautiful-looking Indian receptionist smiled, announced that her boss was expecting them and led them to his office.

"Good morning, Mr. Patel. Thank you for seeing us." Ben shook the mayor's hand.

"The pleasure is mine. What can I do for you?" he said with a grin.

"Let's cut to the chase. You know why I'm here. Leeds is on board, this land needs to be used immediately, and I can make it happen. I've done my research, sir, and it amazes me how two cities 8 miles apart, much like Minneapolis and St Paul's, can't work together. These two cities have worked apart for years, outbidding each other on so many projects. You've both paid too much money in certain deals instead of working as a team. You must start looking at the big picture and that, sir, is the entire county of Yorkshire. This piece of land I would like to acquire is right in the middle of the two cities. It was a crying shame for all your citizens and a disgrace the government did not intervene. Cities and their tax paying citizens should not be scammed by corporate giants. Shit! The company's not even British tax-paying."

Ben paused, looking at the mayor with no facial expression – his poker face.

"Mr. Shannon, this is not so easy. You should know politics play a big part in all of this."

Ben continued without missing a beat, "The one time it worked for both of you was when you co-owned the airport."

Patel interrupted, "What of the airport? Do not remind me. We did not wish to sell; it was the pressure of Leeds and the other councils. It has gone downhill like all the privately owned airports in the UK."

"I know," said Ben, "and the best one, Manchester, is still with the council. Would you like the airport back?"

Patel stood, smoothing the collar of his crisp white shirt. He walked around to Ben. "You now have my attention. Proceed with your proposal, Mr. Shannon."

"I buy the airport for the two cities. Bradford and Leeds control 40% each and my company will have the remaining 20%. In return, you will give me the land near Pudsey absolutely free. My legal team will deal with the company to transfer the rights to me." Before Patel could speak, he continued, "The two cities will each receive 10% of all our revenue earnings at Cougar stadium."

"10% is a little low don't you think?" flashed Patel.

Ben quickly went into his PR mode, "This will be a Disney land in Yorkshire, with concerts, special events, first class restaurants and bars. The Cougars will be the best team in the county and crowds will flock to see the amazing show." He took out a piece of paper from his inside jacket pocket and handed it to Patel, "This is what we are projecting in the next five years."

Patel gaped at the paper for a long moment before saying, "Mr. Shannon. We have a deal."

When they came out of City Hall, Andy gave Ben a high five.

"Boss, that was brilliant! We're on our way to being the top team in the UK."

"Excuse me, Mr. Shannon?" came a voice to Ben's left. He looked to see a young lady running towards him. "Amy Carrington of the *Yorkshire Gazette*. Did you buy the land in Pudsey for your American football team?"

"Well young lady, this is quite a surprise, since it was supposed to be confidential. I intended to announce this to the press this afternoon." Ben brushed past Amy and headed to the limo parked in front. Amy caught up to him.

"Sir, I have just been given a new position with the paper. If you have secured a deal, I will be the new Cougar girl and covering all aspects of the Leeds Cougars."

She watched expectantly while he thought. Ben admired this young lady's tenacity.

"Okay. We have the deal and the city of Leeds is in for a treat."

Ben slid into the back of the limo and pressed the window button.

"What did you say your name is?"

"Amy Carrington," she replied, handing him her business card through the car window.

Chapter 12

Harry, James, and Paul entered the Houston International Airport, all looking up at the departure screen instinctively. Forty-five minutes delay. James decided to head for the bar, suggesting Harry and Paul have some quality time.

"Well, I can't drink so let's get a coffee," said Harry.

They sat at the table, both feeling uneasy with the situation.

"Hey, I want to apologize for the way I treated all the fans outside the hospital and my foul language. I felt weird, like someone else inside my body," Harry said, feeling embarrassed. He recalled that day when his dad and G Pops had picked him up from the hospital.

The crowd outside had heard the news and many of the students had rushed out of university to cheer for him on the hospital grounds. He declined to speak with all the news reporters, looking anxious.

"Get me in the car, Dad. I don't need this," he had said.

G Pops pleaded with him, "Your fans, students, all your good friends have been here for days. Harry, I have spoken with them each of the last five or so nights. "

He waved at them all and with a smile, whispered through his teeth, "G Pops, get me in the fucking car."

That was the first time he had ever used a bad word with

any of the family. He swore like a trooper he reckoned but never with a family member. He did not like his new persona and hoped it would go away once the swelling and bruising had subsided.

"I was more concerned about all those Facebook messages from home. That would make you decide to head back to England."

"Hey, give me some credit. It was all BS and that lot never contacted me once. I can see them now, all sitting in the pub every night, thinking about which subject to moan about next. Maybe I left three years ago and it was my round." He had been surprised with the amount of messages on Facebook from old high school mates that came out of the woodwork with, "Come home; let's have a few pints with the lads," while some girls sent pictures with, "Harry, you are so cute; take me out on a date."

I bet Mum was behind all that.

"Are you getting any flashbacks of the accident, or your time in Texas?" asked Paul.

"The accident is slowly coming back, although all I can remember is still being in the parking lot staring at the ice on the ground. Funny, it continues from there with the recurring nightmare I have had since I was what? Eleven? I am being chased, only I never see the pursuer. Always seem to be on the London Underground, changing stations. It freaks me out."

"I remember, and you never get caught, right?"

"Never. I wake up in a cold sweat way before anybody gets near me."

"What about football?"

"I see me scoring touchdowns, running the ball but never throwing it. How strange is that?"

"Well you did beat the record for most rushing TDs scored by any college QB. It will all come back eventually."

"What about you, G Pops? I guess at your age the nightmares and dreams have stopped."

"Very funny. As a matter of fact I had one last night about you. Well, actually me with your vision appearing at the end."

"Really? Fill me in."

"Okay, you know how well I know Highway 290."

"Like the back of your hand."

"I was driving back from Houston after dropping off you and your dad right here at the airport.

"I know the road better than any. I must have driven this route 500 times or more. With the SUV on cruise, I could regularly glance at Tigger, your cat. I had picked her up from your apartment just like I did after the accident to look after her."

"Thanks for doing that, by the way."

"Hey, this is a dream, mate. May I continue?

"Heading up the incline, I thought to myself, *Down the hill and home in thirty minutes*. I needed a stiff drink or two to take my mind off the day, with you two just leaving for England. As I came to the brow of the hill, the car going down a further gear, there was a sudden downpour of rain to greet me. I had not seen this one black cloud and the rain was beating down on the SUV. I was already heading down the steep hill.

"The vehicle went into a slide – I had lost complete control. Nothing I did made any difference. I tried steering out, touching the brakes – nothing. My mind filled with a song, a song I truly detested. I love Carrie Underwood, hate the song, but now I understood the lyrics and the writer's inspiration for the song. *Jesus, take the wheel*. I suddenly felt more relaxed and literally rested my hands on the wheel and said aloud: 'You decide.'

"The right-hand side was the canyon – a hundred feet drop at least, where I would meet my maker. The left-hand side was a median, long grass, mud from the downpour with a metal barrier. The car spun, spiralling down the hill, seemed it liked the canyon to the right, another spin, and headed left."

"I know exactly where you are," said Harry nodding.

"I came out of my temporary trance. The past week had passed before my eyes.

"In that one second, I saw the future. You were playing football again only I did not recognize the team or the colours and it seemed like you were in England."

"American football? Don't be daft, G Pops. Sure it wasn't cricket?"

"You were wearing a gridiron helmet and shoulder pads! May I finish? I grabbed tightly around the steering wheel, and hit the brakes hard.

"Whoa, Bella! Go left, you bastard! The vehicle powered through the median. I kept the car parallel with the barrier, the long grass and mud slowing the vehicle down. Finally, it came to a stop.

"I took a few minutes to catch my breath as a few cars whizzed by in either direction. 'Okay, then. I guess you've decided I'm worth keeping around,' I said looking up to the skies. I waited for a clear spot and eased out into the road."

"That is weird," said Harry. "I only get part of it: you want me to be the starting QB for the Longhorns and wished the accident never happened. I do too, believe me! The part about being in England is really weird. You see, G Pops, I have no idea why I would want to leave this paradise, my amazing life in Texas. If my family – well except you and Nan – was not in England, I would never leave here.

"Something inside me, a really strong feeling, is telling me going back to England is my destiny!"

Chapter 13

Ben came out of the shower and lay on the bed. Back in his London hotel suite, he felt good about today. He poured a scotch and decided to read this evening rather than watching TV. An early morning flight back and a shit pile of neglected work awaited him tomorrow. A knock at the door surprised him and particularly when he looked through the door spy. He opened the door.

"Denis Bazan in person. What a pleasant surprise."

"All right, mate. How about inviting me in?" Denis was looking cocky with a wide grin on his face.

"How the hell did you get through hotel security?" asked Ben, a tad agitated.

"You are in London, mate – my city. Nothing gets past me. Now are you going to invite me in and offer me a drink?"

He poured two single malts and stared at Denis. "What brings you to my room, hoss?" he said, sarcastically.

"Nice one, mate. You are a strange bird. A Yorkie and Texan all rolled into one and I don't like either fucking one of you. Northern bastards and Texans don't sit well with me, and as for Leeds, I hate 'em. Hate the place – always will. I am a Chelsea fan and remember the old days like yesterday. Fucking Leeds fans came to Stamford Bridge with no colours on, snuck in our end and knifed some of my mates."

Ben looked at him. "So much hate, Denis. That was way back in the seventies."

"1982, actually. I remember that day like it was fucking yesterday. Dirty fucking Leeds fans coming to my manor!"

Denis became agitated, speaking faster, veins bulging from his forehead.

"Oh, but I can go much further back than 1982, mate. How about your family roots in the Ukraine?"

So Denis had hired a genie to make up a complete profile of Ben too.

"A Russian Jew with some Pole thrown in for good measure. I don't like you, Ben Shannon, and I am not happy you found a way in to our BFL, you slimy bastard."

Denis continued to smile while he was talking. Londoners could do that. Smile while they were about to kick the shit out of you, or con you with some scam. At least Northerners were up front and you know well in advance if they were pissed off.

Denis chugged back the remains of his scotch, stood up and put his face an inch from Ben's. "I suggest you go back to rodeo-land tout suite and stay out of my country. Thanks for the scotch." And he was gone.

Ben shook from head to toe and poured another scotch. He lay back on the bed and was sure he would have a restless night. *Fucking prick,* he thought.

Why was it every time he thought about Denis Bazan he became restless, agitated and downright mad? *If he ever comes to Texas I'll shoot him dead*, he thought. *Come into my house for a scotch and I would be in my rights to shoot him. Make sure he was dead and tell the cops he broke into my house. Not guilty verdict every time!* However, this was not Ben. He had not got this far in life by allowing anybody to get under his skin.

He switched on the TV and tuned to highlights of a game: the British football game. *This should take my mind off Denis Bazan.* He smiled and thought about the last season of British premier soccer he had watched on TV at home in Houston. It was 2013 and what an absolute farce! Newcastle, a team he'd always liked as a kid, had seven French players on the pitch for one game. They were completely destroyed: 6-nil by Liverpool at home in St. James Park. Earlier in that year he had watched the new Southampton manager need an interpreter to speak with one of his British players.

If a regular English soccer fan could come to love the French, then there was no doubt in his mind, that American football would become huge in the UK.

"Now I feel better," he said to the TV, finding the remote button to switch it off.

He thought about the upcoming season – all the planning that lay ahead over the next six months. He would have to live half the year in England, expand the UK office. He would have to live in Leeds or close by. Maybe the Yorkshire dales would be a good spot. The preseason would start in March with the first official league game in May. They would have to draft players. Steal them from the Canadian league, since they were paid such a low salary. Build the most amazing stadium.

Yes, much to accomplish this year, and next year – champions. Fill the stadium and show the world.

He slept soundly.

Chapter 14

Amy arrived at the Gazette office at 8:29AM.
The office was filling up fast with staff arriving for work. She could smell strong coffee, hear conversations on a variety of topics. Amy was not accustomed to all this. By the time she got to the office on most days the workers were on their laptops, hard at work. The office went into complete silence as Amy sat down at her desk.

"Amy, did he kick you out of bed early this morning?" came one shout.

"Actually, we had wicked sex about 5AM and then again in the shower." Little did they know she hated men – well, most of the time. Okay, just at the moment.

"Why do you have two coffees?" said another voice. She smiled in their direction while pointing her finger to her nose. No need for any more words with these clowns. She smiled through the window at her boss, tapped on the door and walked in without waiting for an invitation.

"Good morning, sir. A nice Peruvian dark roast and I even remembered to bring you some cream." She placed the large cup on his desk along with a serving of cream and a plastic spoon.

"What the hell is this?" He stared in disbelief. "You have never been on time nor have you ever brought me a coffee in over a year of being in our employment. I hope this isn't going to show up on your expenses. What do you want Amy?"

"Nothing, sir. I just woke up this morning and decided it would be fitting to start treating you with more respect."

"What an absolute load of shite! What do you want?"

"Boss, I have to go to Wembley. It's vital to increase my knowledge of the game. I have arranged an appointment with Ben Shannon and he confirmed. Can you believe that boss?" She smiled smugly. She had, of course, not made an appointment with the very busy Mr. Ben Shannon but she had a plan. Thank God her boss never checked her appointments.

"The readers will enjoy my report on an NFL game. This is top-level American football and not an exhibition game. This is for real, boss. Imagine: Tom Brady's final season."

"Who?"

"Never mind. You'll read all about it in my story. I've asked all my Twitter followers and they agree."

"Twitter? How many followers do you have?"

"I had 1,500 until I became the Cougar girl for you. Now it's over 5,000."

"Very impressive. However, we don't have the budget for you to be spending the weekend in London living up to your normal standards. Hell! The hotels you stay in are better than our CEO gets, and those bloody lunches you have …" He looked at the proposal she had just sent in an email while he was prattling on.

"So your proposal has first-class train travel, two nights in this bloody five-star hotel I have never heard of and the meal allowance you have here is outrageous! And, by the way, thanks for sending me this while I was talking to you. You do piss me off with that damn iPhone: texting and all that twittering."

He pulled up the game information on his large tablet computer, viewing the information he had pulled up on the screen.

"I think you're right. You should go and I am authorizing your trip with a slight alteration. I approve exactly 50% of your request and I suggest you go second class and stay at a comfy B&B. We need a great story, full of excitement and what the fans can expect at the Cougar Dome next year."

Amy left his office and sat at her desk fuming. *What is the matter with him? I do my best work when I am totally relaxed and living in the lap of luxury. Well he said 50% and I have not had a break in ages. I will pay for half myself and find a way to get it back later!*

Chapter 15

Paul boarded the train at London Paddington for the one-hour train journey to Kemble. Once at Kemble it was a short taxi ride to his son's house where Harry had been staying ever since the accident in Texas.

There had been no contact from either party, which bothered Paul to no end. It was the pride thing yet again.

He began to sing a song, making sure there was no one in earshot. *"Passion or coincidence once prompted you to say: Pride will tear us both apart. Well now pride's gone out the window, cross the rooftops, run away. Left me in the vacuum of my heart."*

He smiled, reminiscing his days as a New Romantic back in the early eighties which always made him happy, glad to be back in England. His favorite band was Duran Duran. He had all their albums, had been to many concerts back then and even last year. He was so shocked to see them perform last year, but they still had it after all that time. He drifted into a daydream with the countryside flashing by and the gentle sound of the train.

He had never forgotten the last comment from Harry: my destiny is back in England. Doing what? He had mulled it over in his mind. Harry without football was unimaginable with all that talent. He had racked his brain for weeks, finally stumbling on an idea after browsing the Internet – Harry's idol, Tom Brady. Destiny, fate or whatever one called our path in life – Brady had experienced it. Being a sixth round pick and backup for Drew Bledsoe, there never seemed to be a chance Brady would become the starting QB. Bledsoe was the golden boy, picked first overhaul in the 1993 draft. The Patriots gave him a record deal in 2001 of 103 million dollars for the next ten years, a true commitment that he would be their leader until his retirement. Unfortunately the next season he was injured, never regaining his starting position. Meanwhile, Brady was so good, taking them to a Super Bowl win, and to this day he'd never been replaced.

Accidents are in your stars – they happen for a reason. Sometimes they have a positive impact on your life, other times they don't.

He came back with a jolt just as the train was stopping in Kemble. He had sent a text in advance to the local taxi company and they actually remembered him. "You're Harry's granddad! It's been a while since we last saw you. Not a problem sir."

Paul climbed out of the taxi, rang the doorbell and was shocked to see Harry open the door.

"G Pops!" Harry gave him a big hug. "I have been meaning to phone you."

"Me too," said Paul.

"Does Dad know you were coming?" Harry looked confused.

"No, I wanted to surprise you is all. Where is everybody?"

"At a family get-together up in Yorkshire. They won't be back until after the weekend. Anyway, sit yourself down and I will make us a brew."

Harry brought in two big mugs of tea.

After a moment of silence, Paul decided it was time to shit or get off the pot.

"Harry, I have a present for you." He gave him the envelope. Harry pulled out the ticket and looked at it.

"Why are you so hell-bent on me playing football, G Pops?"

"Before you moan, hear me out. Since you're the only British QB ever to play at a US college, I don't think your talent should go to waste."

"Do you mean all the time you spent with me, making me so good?"

"Of course not! They were special times for me, I must admit. So what do you think about your present?"

"Not interested," he muttered. He put the ticket down and headed for the kitchen to find some biscuits.

"You saw it was the Patriots right?"

"Not interested, for the last time."

"Tom Brady's final season and the last time here in the UK."

Harry said nothing and pulled out an iPad from under the sofa cushion. He studied the screen and could see this was indeed Brady's last.

This was to be Brady's final season, his last chance to beat the one record that he still tied with Montana and Bradshaw. All three players had four Super Bowl wins, but Brady was hungry for five. After that, Brady already had the rest.

"I like it, except for your ulterior motive to get me playing again." He paused to think, then sighed. "We'll go. But, G Pops: no pressure, agreed?"

They shook on it and had another big bear hug.

"You do know my Mum and Dad will have something to

say about your surprise visit and the two of us going to Wembley tomorrow."

"I know." He sighed.

"Just assure them this is not in any way a trick to get me back to Texas."

Chapter 16

The streets were lined with fans going down to Wembley Stadium.

There seemed to be every colour imaginable, all teams represented by the thousands of British fans with allegiances for the most diverse reasons. Bradford City fans had always followed Washington because of their similar club colours. Miami was for all the cruise holidaymakers. New York, Chicago and California teams were from favorite TV shows. The Patriots had been before. In the game versus the St Louis Rams, which the Pats won easily, the Rams had been the home team and yet the stadium was full of Patriots fans. The Rams' coach did say, "We might be the home team, but after all they are named the New *England* patriots."

Whatever their allegiance, today was Patriot day and the New Orleans Saints fans were hard to find.

They found their seats early enough to watch the players warming up.

"Look at Brady! That throwing action looks the same as sseventeen years ago." Paul was so excited to have Harry by his side, football hopefully back in his life.

Harry said nothing and kept watching Brady. Three steps back, fire, a tight spiral piercing through the air like a small missile, into the hands of the receiver. It was a sight to witness. They had a celebration for him just before the game.

Brady's first Super Bowl win in 2001 replayed on all the giant screens around the stadium.

Half-time was to be some new kid: the next Canadian superstar, along with a video link back to Boston with a special mystery guest to perform a tribute for all of Brady's accomplishments.

The game was the usual nip and tuck, the same as whenever the Patriots played the Saints. Both teams were excellent on offence. By half-time the score was tied at 14-14. Brady looked good.

"Hey, G Pops, mind if I walk around on my own for a while?"

"Sure. I'll get myself a beer."

Paul was standing in line at one of the bars when he saw an old friend. He was the offense coach for UT. Paul literally ran over to him like a running back, avoiding tackles through the crowd of people.

"John! How the hell are you?" Paul gave him a high five.

"We all miss Harry at UT. How is he doing?"

"He's here at the game – seems to perking up and never took his eyes off Brady."

"I have tickets for the VIP lounge. Why don't you and Harry come after the game and we'll catch up?"

"You bet," said Paul enthusiastically.

Paul headed back to his seat. Harry took his seat on the first drive of the second half. He looked focused and quiet. By the end of third quarter the Saints were up 28-14.

"The Patriots look out of it," Paul said. "I think your boy is getting tired. It can't be easy playing this game, in that position, at 40-years-old."

Harry gave his granddad a quick squeeze on the shoulder. "There's a quarter left. Never count Brady out, G Pops."

They watched that final quarter in total amazement. True to Harry's word, the Patriots came back, seemingly scoring at random.

At the final whistle, the score was 42-28. Five touchdowns had been Brady's work.

"You were right. Now let's go upstairs. I have someone that wants to meet you."

"Upstairs? G Pops, you promised."

Paul held up his hands. "No tricks. Don't worry."

Chapter 17

Once in the lounge with a beer in hand, Paul watched a guy chatting to a group. He looked excited, arms flapping, explaining something that was obviously emotional to him. Harry was busy talking to his coach, John Nixon, hearing all the scoop from UT.

"Who is that?" Paul asked John.

"Ben Shannon, the owner of the Leeds Cougars."

"Leeds Cougars are back?"

"Yeah. They bought Sheffield and moved the franchise to Leeds. Seems their giant dome stadium will be ready for next season. Would you like to meet him?"

A thought occurred in Paul's mind. "Yes we would."

John waited for the right moment. Ben had calmed down and was nodding continuously while listening to a group of people. John and Paul slowly moved over to the group.

"Excuse me, Ben. I'd like to introduce you to an old friend of mine, Paul Smith."

They shook hands and Ben asked if he had enjoyed the game.

"Yes. I have my grandson with me, and it could be turning point for him."

"Turning point?" Ben asked.

"Harry …" Paul began, unsure how to explain everything.

He glanced at Harry, who gazed out of the window over the field, lost in thought.

Ben followed his eyes, stopped him, squeezed his arm. "Harry Smith, the former QB for UT?"

Paul smiled, looking over at Harry.

"Goddamn! It was all over the news in Texas. How the hell is the boy doing?" he asked with some emotion in his voice.

"It's been a tough year and I never thought he would come today. He hasn't taken his eyes off Brady since we got here, which has to be a good sign."

Ben signaled to one of the waiting staff. Paul called Harry over and they all moved to a large table in the corner.

"Harry, I would like you to meet Mr. Shannon."

"Call me Ben. I've heard a lot about your career at UT. I was free safety at Houston in my day and never miss a home game. I saw what you did to our team last season. It's not often we have UT come to town, and completely dominate a game on our own turf. You scored three touchdowns if my memory serves me well?"

"That was a good game. I did play well that day. Actually, I feel like I have met you before. I saw your videos and pictures in a business study I did in school. We featured your company as a business model at the university a couple of years back."

Harry and Ben continued to chat, with Paul and John watching the two of them. They touched on many aspects of American football. Paul was content just listening to Harry. His enthusiasm for the game had returned after such a rough year.

A young lady approached Ben from behind, and coughed to get his attention. He turned to her with delayed recognition, then stood from the table and shook her hand.

"Gentlemen, meet Amy Carrington from the *Yorkshire Gazette*," Ben announced.

He pulled back a chair, which Amy took and thanked him.

"How the hell did you get in here?" Ben scrutinized her clearance pass, which certainly looked like a fake. "Never mind. You're a ballsy young lady. I'd like you to meet my guests, Paul and Harry Smith, and John Nixon, offense coach at UT. Gentlemen, this is our Cougar girl who will be reporting on the Leeds Cougars' first season, all the way to our bowl win. Isn't that right Amy?"

"Yes. We already have Cougar fever in Yorkshire. Is there anything I can tell our readers and Twitter followers, Mr. Shannon?"

"Amy Carrington, let me buy you a drink," Ben said. "What will it be?"

"May I look at the wine list, Mr. Shannon?"

"Certainly. And, please, call me Ben."

She took the wine list from him and looked eagerly. Paul had to laugh at her boldness. More intriguing was Harry's interested stare. He hadn't seemed interested in girls since his accident.

"Amy, are you going to read the menu from top to bottom? Would you like me to pick a suitable wine?"

"Absolutely not! Sorry, that came out rude. I know about wine, quite passionate about it really and I have a dilemma. I really want the Chateau Sancerre but they don't have it by the glass, in fact the selection is quite poor for wines by the glass."

Ben called the waiter. "Please bring me a bottle of the Chateau Sancerre, ice bucket and five glasses. Is the wine slightly chilled?" He turned to his guests confidentially. "Most people drink their white wine far too cold."

"Yes, sir. I believe it is 11 degrees."

"That's 52 Farenheit, right? That's just fine."

"I will bring it immediately." The waiter hurried away.

"I am a bit of a wine collector myself. Amy, that wine is a perfect choice. Now let me just change the subject for a second. Harry, will you sign for the Cougars?"

Paul held his breath, watching Harry for his response.

"I know you had a dreadful accident and there is no pressure. We have our eyes on a star QB out of the USA and you would be our backup. We could see how you go. Take all the time you need with your comeback."

The entire table waited, spellbound, to hear Harry's answer. Paul looked at Harry, willing him to say yes. In his peripheral, Ben and Amy looked just as eager.

The moment was broken by a deep London accent.

"Ben Shannon! As I live and breathe. How are you, mate?" A man with a Cheshire-cat-like smile stood over them.

Ben, with a pasted-on grin, made the rounds of introduction. "Folks, this is Denis Bazan, owner of the London Ravens."

Denis looked once, couldn't believe his eyes, and looked again in the direction of Harry. "Harry Smith, the British quarterback that played for Texas? What a shame about the accident, mate. All washed up and nowhere to go. I imagine

Ben here is trying to persuade you to come out of retirement and play for the Cougars next season? And who is this lovely darling?" He undressed Amy with his shifty dark brown eyes.

"Amy Carrington of the *Yorkshire Gazette*, and the official reporter for the Leeds Cougars," she announced proudly, though she pulled her hand away from his as soon as she could.

"Well, Amy, I look forward to your first report on the season opener at the bloody Cougar Dome, if it's ready on time. 'Ravens destroy Cougars.' Washed-up Harry Smith is a perfect fit for a bunch of Leeds tossers."

Paul leapt up from the table, planning to head straight for Denis. Ben stopped him just in time and whispered, "He's not worth it."

"That was fun." Denis paused, grinning wickedly. "Nice to meet you too, Granddad. I'll see you around."

Two big guys appeared out of nowhere and flanked Denis. One said, "Everything all right, Mr. Bazan? "

"Yeah. I was just saying goodbye to these lovely people." And with that he was gone.

Amy took a sip of wine. "That guy gave me the creeps. We'd better beat his bloody marvelous Ravens."

Ben nodded. "We will."

"I'd like to help you do that, Mr. Shannon," Harry suddenly announced. "I'll sign with your team."

Perfect timing. Paul's mood lifted for the first time since Harry's accident. They all raised their glasses to the announcement.

PART 2

Chapter 18

Six months later

Harry wove his way through a set of tires laid out on the training ground, his feet moving fast. *Don't miss one*, he kept telling himself. Through the last set and *bam* he hit the blocking dummy as hard as he could. He fell on the ground, panting, sweating and his body aching from head to foot.

Harry continued panting, his face buried in the muddy ground. He was wearing a huge football helmet which caused his head to sweat, while the rest of his body had already turned cold. It was a miserable day in Leeds with the weather still in its usual winter mode, somehow ignoring the fact it was spring.

But it was only the first day at training camp. The Cougars had assembled some of the finest players from the Canadian Football League, with a scattering of players from Europe, with even an Aussie trying out for field goal kicker. Some were in shape while others took turns to go puke on the sidelines. At that moment, Harry felt decidedly sick. He was so out of shape after a year off. Through his spinning head, he heard the sound of other players gagging.

"Harry Smith, get your lazy ass up right now. Running on the spot until I tell you stop."

"Yes, Coach."

Harry ran on the spot reluctantly while fully appreciating all the physical demands imposed at training camp, is the first step to becoming champions! He recalled the first team meeting earlier in the day with all the coaches. Their first priority at training camp was to build up stamina, followed by stretching which included the neck roll to help avoid any nasty injuries.

Football players hit with their helmets on, with lethal force. They needed a strong neck, especially the quarterbacks. Although quarterbacks don't have to hit that often, most times they are the one being hit. *A QB never got out of any exercise at training camp, no matter how much you try to fool them,* he thought. It paid dividends throughout the season but he would do anything to get out of this first day.

"This is a team sport and all players are striving to be one supreme unit without a single flaw," the coaches repeated at their meeting. He detested the stamina exercises. They were so tough often lasting three hours per session.

He continued to think, taking his mind off the pain, his heart beating so fast, his legs feeling like weights. The non-American players would be fighting it out for a few spots to play on special teams. At this level some of the starters were expected to play the kick and punt returns. However, the more a team could keep the stars away from special team duty, the better. Some of the hardest hitting dudes play for that solitary minute, only on a few occasions per game when there is a punt or kickoff, with the sole purpose of causing bodily damage to the opponents. They gather up speed running half of the field and hit you like a high-speed train that lost its brakes.

The sound of the whistle was music to Harry's ears. *Blessed release! Now please tell me I can throw some balls.*

"Brad, take the offensive linemen and running backs. Harry, throw short passes to the slot receivers. Roll out left and right in the read option style," shouted one of the coaches.

He rolled right three times with good passes to the receiver who was told to run a 10 and out pattern. Harry put the ball in the correct space, only to watch the receivers miss the ball. They seemed totally out of sync, running out of bounds without the ball. He repeated the exercise to the left – same thing.

"Receivers, we are not in Canada now!" yelled the coach. Harry understood. CFL pitches were 10 yards wider and he would have to work on better timing with them. He thought about the problem, his mind flashing back to his early days at Texas.

His coach had explained, "If you watch this game on the TV, it looks like the QB throws directly to the receiver. No, son. That is why you have a playbook – so each player knows exactly where to be with any given play. You're throwing into space. The receiver should know where to be, and they should turn exactly at the right moment – the ball right there in their hands."

He tried again with the receivers, which resulted in about a 50% completion rate. Not good enough.

The coach instructed Brad and Harry to swap roles with Harry now working with the backs. That proved to be a disaster. He could not get the plays down. He looked over at Brad who was now throwing balls in long, medium and short passes. *Man, he is good!*

With the first full practice behind him, his body aching so badly, he slowly walked over to G Pops who had been watching practice, a video recorder in hand.

"Never thought you would come to opening-day practice. I bet we all looked terrible."

"Hey, I have nothing better to do and I thought you may need to take a look at yourself. It's been over a year."

"It feels more like five! I need a long shower. See you later," he shouted, heading for the dressing rooms.

Chapter 19

What a sight! Amy had never seen exercise drills like this. She asked one of the coaches what was going on.

"Calisthenics," he replied. She would check that word on Google later.

A coach shouted, "Jumping jacks!" and blew his whistle. She watched in amazement at forty players all in their full gridiron uniforms doing a routine that looked more suited to dance – all of them together in unison.

The coach yelled that the next exercise in their routine was "ups and downs". Amy was trying to recall if she had ever seen anything like this one. They would go down on the ground, jump back up, with their bodies frozen like a deer in the headlights. The only part of the body moving was their legs and feet. Feet moving fast like a tap dancer. She moved around the back of the players, ready to take interesting shots with her Canon camera from a variety of angles. This would be great for the blog.

Suddenly, she noticed a player wearing the #12 jersey: Harry Smith. His feet moved fast on the spot. *Now, what a bloody gorgeous sight, his ass in those tight pants*, she thought playfully.

Enough of all this, it's making me exhausted just watching them, she thought after thirty minutes of snapping shots and taking notes.

She noticed an elderly gentleman standing on the sidelines taking notes. Older than her dad, perhaps early sixties. *Wait a minute. That's Harry's granddad. I met him at Wembley.* She strolled over to speak with him, keeping her recent thought of number 12 firmly under wraps.

"Good morning, sir. I'm Amy Carrington of the *Yorkshire Gazette*. We met briefly at Wembley when Harry agreed to sign for the Cougars."

"I remember. Paul Smith," he said, shaking her hand heartily.

"You seem a bit down in the dumps," she said, shivering. "I know the weather is diabolical for this time of the year."

"It's not so bad. You know, I've admired your stories. Since we met I've been reading the *Gazette* and your articles online: 'Leeds Cougars sign Prince Harry.' I cried, actually, when I first saw you make reference to 'Prince Harry'. I was so proud when he was first tagged with that nickname in Texas. You'd better be careful here with the real prince in the news. They could sue you or something."

She laughed. "Don't worry, Mr. Smith. We have our legal cover those issues. I just use it for fun, really, and I did make reference to the Texas origin."

She sized him up. Was he ready for some questions? She decided to give it a go. "Do you think you could answer some questions about Harry for me?"

"Could I buy you a cup of tea?" Paul Smith offered.

"I'm not much of a tea girl, but coffee would be good. And please, it's my treat. I insist." Amy linked his arm and walked to the café. She bought a coffee for herself and a tea for Paul, and they sat at a tall table where they could still see the field.

"Well, Mr. Smith – " she stirred a packet of sugar in her coffee " – I've read as much as I can about Harry, playing for Texas University and the serious accident. I was hoping you could fill in some of the gaps for me. I do know you had a part to play in developing his special skills and passion for American football."

"Well, that is a long story, young lady. How about I give you the shorter version?"

"Sounds great." Amy held up a voice recorder with a questioning eyebrow, and Paul nodded. She pressed record and put it on the table.

"We lived close to an American air force base in Cirencester. Back in my day it was full of Americans. In fact, it was regarded as American soil, so I needed a special pass to get through security. American football was the big thing there, of course. I had become friends with a football coach, studied the game, finally having the opportunity to become an assistant coach.

"Those American kids were damn good. I never pushed Harry to become interested in the game. One day he was with me at training, not more than twelve-years-old, watching my buddy throw the ball to receivers. Harry walked up, asked if he could have a go. Coach showed him how to hold the ball with his fingers on the laces, shouted to one of the kids, 'Go on a 10 and out.' The kid shot downfield 10 yards, made the cut to the outside. Harry fired the ball straight into his hands like a dart. It was effortless and so precise. He trained at the base for quite a few years but he never played a game.

"Once at the University of Texas, football was the furthest from his mind. He wanted to be in banking. Had done since he was 5-years-old." Paul paused for a second, his emotions getting the better of him. "By the time he was seven he would have a book with all his deposits logged of all the money he had received from birthdays, Christmas, etc. He never spent any of his own savings, relying on his dad for spending money. The penny dropped – no pun intended – when a few years later he loaned his dad fifty pounds. It was some kind of emergency when James could not get to a bank. A year later, Harry asked for the money back with an additional 10% interest."

Amy laughed. Harry, a numbers guy. Interesting.

"In his second year at UT, the team had a series of injuries – all three of their QB's. Harry bumped into the coach at some function and mentioned he could throw a ball. The coach never took him seriously, making an acceptable assumption that no British lad could play football. I mean, their football game. But they got desperate and he got a call to come down and throw a few balls at practice. The rest is history. In his third year, Harry broke all records, with the distinction of beating an old record for any QB running in touchdowns. The fans gave him the title 'Prince Harry'." Paul stopped suddenly, tears in his eyes. Amy reached across the table and squeezed his hand.

"His accident must have been hard for you."

"It was hard for all of us. Honestly, football was the farthest thing from any of our minds, until we knew he'd be okay."

"Now, you had something to do with getting him interested in football again, didn't you, Mr. Smith?"

He ducked his head, smiling. "I can't take the credit for that. I just got the tickets to the Patriots game. He became interested again thanks to his idol Tom Brady. That game at Wembley really got his juices flowing. Signing with the Cougars has rekindled all his passion."

Passion for more than football, Amy hoped.

"Now we just need to see him succeed in training camp."

A shadow passed over Paul's face. "If he could just find that second that seems to be missing, then he would have a chance to push Brad hard to be starting QB by the opening game of the season."

"I hope so, too. Thank you for speaking with me, Mr. Smith." Amy stood and switched off her recorder, then reached across the table to shake Paul's hand.

He smiled for the first time today, his face radiant. "This is more than just professional interest for you, isn't it?"

Amy froze, like a kid caught with her hand in the cookie jar.

"Don't worry. I think you would be good for him. I could tell you quite liked him when we met at Wembley."

"I … I thought he had a girlfriend," she said, smiling curiously.

"He did, but you know what long-distance relationships are like. Her name is Kelly and they were pretty happy. But Harry changed after the accident. Even my strong bond with him became very weak and I imagine the same can be said regarding Kelly."

"Are they still serious?"

"Not since the accident. I don't think they're even talking these days."

"Just between us," Paul continued, "the two of you would make a great team, once Harry builds up the nerve to ask you out."

Chapter 20

"Hey, G Pops! Get out the plates! I am absolutely starving!"

Harry had stopped off at the local fish and chip shop, which was around the corner from his granddad's flat. Paul had rented the flat on the outskirts of Leeds on a six month lease. Harry's nan had apparently been very understanding and said she would pop over for a couple of the games once the season got started.

Harry loved his fish and chips, particularly in Yorkshire where they used haddock over cod. Paul pulled out two ales from the fridge.

"Brilliant! A feast fit for a king!" Harry licked his lips. Harry opened the can, took a long drink, picked up his knife and fork and tucked into the meal like it would be his last.

"Oh these are so good! The chap at the shop said he was doing the big crunchy batter again. It seems like the place got closed down the last time, breaking EU laws. He started back up and the place is chock-a-block full every night. He said ballocks to the EU laws. He's right, G Pops; if we want cholesterol, we should be allowed. Make our fucking decisions in what we eat, right?"

"Well this is it for you this week, lad. You'll feel it in training tomorrow."

Harry grabbed two more ales out of the fridge, handing

one to Paul in the living room. Paul had a large screen TV and a smaller 22-inch which was rigged up to his video recorder.

"Okay. Watch this," he said while pressing play on the smaller screen remote player. Harry watched intently.

That can't be me, he thought. *I'm bloody awful.*

"What do you think of yourself?" asked Paul, looking serious.

"Very rusty."

Paul flicked the remote, changing to the big screen with a Texas game coming into view. Harry was behind the center. He faked to the running back, changing the play, keeping the ball, running upfield, touchdown!

Man, I was good, thought Harry, evoking memories of that special year.

"The difference, Harry, is you didn't hesitate back then, or think twice. You just went out and did it. You're overthinking at practice."

"I know. I can't seem to focus completely. Can we change the subject? I've seen enough. Maybe you can keep analyzing and give me pointers. Right now, I can't bear to see myself at practice." He changed the subject like a swerving car.

"I noticed you chatting with the reporter today. Where did the two of you go?"

"We had a spot of tea and a right old chinwag."

"Really, what? About your old days?"

"Something like that. But mainly about you."

"Great. I hope not too much about my glory days. I don't need any more pressure right now."

"Well, Harry, the pressure is all around you, probably

more intense than Texas. You were after all a big surprise at UT, technically their fourth choice. Cougar fans love the fact you're from England, even if it is the South." He smiled. "We have all these talented Americans, and Shannon with his enormous Cougar Dome. The fans will get behind the team for sure. However, you would be the very large icing on the cake. An English lad leading their team would be extra special."

"Bloody hell! When you put it like that … Best get home and show up with my A game at practice in the morning."

Harry got to the door and turned.

"So, she mentioned me, right?"

"Oh. We're back on Amy, are we?" He chuckled. "Of course she did. You need to ask her out."

"Shit! A gorgeous girl like her in my head is all I need right now. One thing at a time, G Pops! Thanks for the chat."

"My door is always open for you. Always has been, always will."

Chapter 21

Ben had called the first official coaches meeting of the season to ascertain which players may be cut and if any new players were needed. He was fully aware that training camp usually gave the coaches a good indication of who would make the team and if their offense and defense philosophy would work. Ben looked around the room at all the various charts on the wall, and the coaches with laptops. Videos of all the drills and plays from training camp were playing. It was a hive of activity.

"Well, guys, let's have an assessment after the first two weeks of camp." The head coach stood holding a clipboard in his hand. "Defense is excellent, no problem in that department. We are still working on special teams. We have a few lads from Europe that know how to hit, great tacklers with their rugby background. The Aussie lad should be our kicker, although he makes me nervous with his accuracy. He has one hell of a leg, kicking 60 yards in practice without any effort. On offense, we have a good unit. Brad is coming along by leaps and bounds. Leroy has an attitude, but great talent. Only problem is he has no chemistry with Brad, who never seems to throw him the ball."

"Harry?" Ben inquired.

"Shit. Mr. Shannon, I don't think he'll make the team."

The room went quiet, the coaches all fixed on Ben, waiting for a response.

"Harry was my pick; let me think on that one. In the meantime we have the doc here to assess all the players. Doc Shackleton comes highly recommended as a sports psychologist working with famous soccer stars, golfers and the like. I know it's not easy for some of our players to adapt to our lifestyle in England and being away from their families. Doc will give us some good advice on how to best deal with these problems. I did ask him to spend more time with Harry. Let's wait for his assessment before we make any hasty decisions."

Ben went back into his office. *Shit. Harry is so good for building the fan base. What the fuck am I going to do with him?*

Chapter 22

Amy had a phone call. She had just finished reading her own article in the *Gazette* on Harry. She had written Paul's short story word for word, with an emphasis on how the "Prince" first picked up a ball and his rise to fame in Texas.

She checked her iPhone display. Cougar office, it said. *Shit*, she thought. *Stay cool and professional.*

"Amy Carrington. Good morning."

"Amy? Janice here, Mr. Shannon's personal assistant. Would you pop by please? He would like a word."

"Certainly. What time?"

"Right away would be perfect."

"Okay. I'll be there in no time."

She had just got ready for work wearing her usual pants, hair tied back in a ponytail and her flat cap. *Bloody hell! Well, this is how I go to work, and I need to get my ass over there fast.* "Hey girl, stop worrying about how you look for Mr. Shannon. This is me by day, take or leave it," she said out loud.

She jumped into her Mini Cooper sports and sped down to the ring road to enter the dual carriageway for Pudsey. She loved her car. Good thing small sporty cars were back in style, along with a regular diesel engine. Those poxy environmentally-friendly cars were so slow and what did it matter anyway? When the world all turned "green", they'd had the coldest winters in years with piles of snow. Greenhouse was just a load of hype.

She had been so surprised that a good-looking multi-millionaire had taken a shine to her. He was old enough to be her dad, but he was hot for his age and a really good person to have on her side. Shit, she was the Cougar girl and the owner liked her. *I will milk this wherever possible.*

She arrived in reception where Janice shook her hand and showed her straight into Ben Shannon's office. "Good morning, Miss Carrington. Please take a seat," said Ben with a wide smile. "I've just read your article in the Gazette this morning."

"Me too. It's a bloody good one, wouldn't you say?"

Ben smiled.

"Well, Amy, I found it very entertaining. My problem is that your story is focusing a bit too much on 'Prince Harry, the British QB.' That's all well and good if he makes it through training camp! Otherwise it could be a PR nightmare. Amy, do you have a plan B?"

"Not really. I expect Harry will be our QB star. Paul Smith is super confident he will come round." She stretched the truth a tad.

Ben Shannon glared at her, tapping his fingers on the desk.

"Okay, Mr. Shannon. I do have a plan B."

"Will you enlighten me?"

She smiled like Mona Lisa. "No. Just leave it with me."

"You are a confident young lady. Is that the Yorkshire in you?"

"It's always been the way I roll. Plenty of courage."

"You mean attitude?" he chuckled. "Are your family from Yorkshire?"

"Well, the Carringtons are one of the oldest families in Yorkshire, but I think my attitude is down to the mixture of both sides of my family."

"You look a touch Spanish."

"Italian, actually, on my mother's side. She was born in a small region at the southern tip of Italy, just across from the Island of Sicily."

Ben knew the area from his extensive wine knowledge. "Primitivo country if I am not mistaken."

"Bang on, Mr. Shannon! I forgot you're a wine connoisseur."

"Speaking of which…" Ben handed Amy an envelope. "…why don't you pop by tomorrow evening?"

She opened a white envelope to find an invitation to Ben Shannon's residence. *A housewarming get-together*.

"Bring a friend if you like."

"No thanks. I'll be okay on my own. I'll enjoy some quality time with quality wine for a change. My dad got me hooked on wine and, no, I am not inviting him."

"No boyfriend?"

"I do have a boyfriend. He just doesn't know it yet!"

Ben's eyebrows shot up and he laughed.

Amy, be professional. "To change the subject, do you think I could I have a quote while I am here?" She got her recorder ready.

"Why certainly, and quite relevant to our conversation. My quote is: *Our starting QB Brad Douglas is taking the majority of the reps and looking extremely sharp in training camp. We do expect*

Harry Smith will be the backup QB. All successful football teams have two strong quarterbacks. The Cougar Dome is on schedule and will be fully operational for the season opener when we play the reigning champions, the London Ravens. Tickets are available and I encourage everybody in Yorkshire to make it a family day. We guarantee you will be highly entertained. End quote."

"Thanks so much, Mr. Shannon. If that will be all, I'd better get writing."

"Of course. Goodbye, Miss Carrington. And don't forget about my little party."

Chapter 23

Amy was looking hot parading around her bedroom, if she did say so herself.

Still, it was a difficult decision, what to wear for this party tonight. She had changed three times and was now wearing a tight dress with her long hair hanging over one shoulder.

"Wow girl, you would pull a guy tonight for sure," she said in her low fake sexy voice while dancing in front of the mirror. She turned away, feeling foolish.

She hid her beauty from most people, always wanting to impress for her intellect, savvy street-smarts and confidence. Her reticence really was her parents' fault. When she had turned sixteen she was allowed to go to the parties and wine get-togethers with her parents' friends.

Her mum would always remark, "Amy, my belle, you look so much like Sophia Loren." It was so embarrassing that finally she and her mates had checked pictures of the actress. All agreed back in her day Sophia was a stunner.

Liz, her best friend, had studied the pictures very seriously, "Amy you have a similar mouth, the lips, but that is about all you have in common. Where is your mum looking? You have nicer eyes and nose. In fact, you are more beautiful than her." *Now, that is a best mate*, she had thought at the time.

Loren's biography had revealed that she had been born

in Naples. No wonder her mum was convinced of the similarity. She was so biased for Italy it made Amy wonder how she could still be here in Yorkshire. *She loves Dad and me and just puts up with the shitty weather*, she decided. Like Loren, her mum was born just outside Naples.

"No one ever talked about her being clever, did they Mum?" she said aloud to her reflection. "Look where beauty and sex appeal got Marilyn Monroe."

No. If anyone was going to love Amy, it was for who she was, not what she looked like.

She decided on a more conservative outfit, with trousers and a jacket, ordered a taxi and took a ride to a large gated home. She paid the fare and pressed the button on the gate.

A well-spoken male voice asked her name.

"Amy Carrington."

"Yes, please, come in."

She walked up the long driveway, which had a distinctive smell of roses and some other heady scents she didn't recognize. She stopped at the bottom of the steps to admire the house. A tall elderly gentleman opened the door.

"Miss Carrington? Welcome to the Shannon residence. Please, come in."

Two huge, impressive white columns flanked the door at the top of the marble stone steps. Once inside the house – Ben Shannon's new house – she strained her neck looking at the vaulted ceilings. The skylights were so high you'd need a telescope just to enjoy a view, never mind the stars. How would you clean them? This was a smaller scale version of the Cougar Dome. A monument to a man's ego. Ben Shannon knew how to live.

A tap on her shoulder brought her out of her admiration. She turned to see Ben dressed in expensive jeans and an open white shirt.

"Thank you for coming, Amy. You are looking quite businesslike this evening. I should have emphasized we are always smart casual at the Shannon house. That means jeans." His friendly smile banished her embarrassment. "I have some guests to speak with, so why don't you have a walk around and help yourself to a drink? I'll show you the start of my wine collection later and you can pick a bottle. I have some excellent '97 vintage. However, all my older wines are back in Houston."

He left her alone with a friendly touch on the shoulder, and she took his invitation to wander off. Inwardly she was kicking herself that she hadn't chosen a more casual outfit. After all, it was just a housewarming party. She checked out all of the downstairs area. Each room had a giant TV screen with its own music genre streaming via airplay. One had classic rock – right now it was Mick & Keith live somewhere in the US. One room was pop and a quiet room at the back of the house was playing soft jazz. She walked over to a long bar where a young bartender with a hideous handlebar moustache was handing out drinks.

"Good evening. May I interest you in a special cocktail? We use only local organic ingredients and my expertise is the classics.

"Actually, I am more of a wine girl. However, you have piqued my interest. I like a G & T occasionally."

"I can elaborate on that with my own creation." The bartender went to work adding a splash of this, a twist of that, shaking his concoction and pouring it smoothly into a glass with a garnish of lemon and a blackberry on a pick. "I guarantee you'll like it. A Bramble cocktail – it's my own creation." He presented it like a culinary masterpiece, his eyes alight with arrogance.

Amy watched the blackberry liqueur slowly slide through the ice cubes. It was such a spectacle in the glass, she decided to resist the temptation to drink it for a few moments. Then she met the bartender's eyes over the rim of the glass as she sipped.

"This is delicious. You certainly know your cocktails."

"Thank you, madam. I do."

Egotistical bastard. She moved on to view the fine art in the room.

She made light conversation for a few hours with many of the guests. Some were quite interested in the Cougars, making complimentary comments on her articles in the Gazette.

Many of the guys were indeed wearing smart jeans with expensive open-necked shirts. Most of the ladies were following the latest fashion. Short tight skirts were back in style, once again. She had bought several this past month and would show off her great legs on Thursday night in the city. *I'll turn a few heads.* She smiled. *In the meantime, I need to mingle wearing this lame outfit. Girl, what were you thinking?*

She did find one lovely couple. He was one of the main Cougar sponsors with a large communications company. He gave her his card and promised to let her write a piece on his fascination for the Cougars and his decision to support them this season. His wife was really friendly, remarking that her teenage son was following Amy on Twitter.

Finally Ben said goodbye to the last guest and headed for the cocktail bar.

"Well, Amy, what do you think of the new homestead? Let me get a cocktail and we can check out my new wine collection."

They moved down the spiral staircase into a modern style wine cellar, which featured a new state-of-the-art temperature control system. There was a full range of 1997 wines from California and Italy.

"What is through this door?" She pointed to a heavy, sealed door.

"The whites and champagne are kept slightly cooler."

"Nice touch."

"Pick one."

Amy studied the reds, feeling a bit like a kid in a candy store, finally choosing a Raymond Cabernet Sauvignon from Napa Valley.

"I haven't heard of this one. What do you think?"

"Not the best I have, but a good choice. It's very easy on the palette. I said it would be your choice, so let's give it a try."

He decanted the wine, poured a small serving in each glass. "Give it a big swirl first. I'll top off your glass once you have a taste."

Amy gave him the evil eye.

"My apologies. I had forgotten your family is into wine. Of course you know what to do."

Amy nosed and then took a gentle sip, taking the wine back in her mouth and breathing in through her teeth before she swallowed.

"Cedar and currants on the nose, very Bordeaux on the palette, pure velvet. I like it," she said confidently.

"Okay, enough about wine. I know when to fold my hand." He filled the glasses and took a sip. "Let's change the subject. I asked you yesterday about the Carrington family name, with your mother being Italian. I have a good friend that runs a genealogy company. If I had time I would take it up as a hobby."

It seemed as though this was slightly more than a hobby for him.

"Well, I do know we are an old Yorkshire family as I mentioned to you in your office. My uncle had a wicked Yorkshire accent. It sounded so foreign. Research has shown it's the oldest in England, coming from the Vikings. Not so popular now in England, but I keep seeing the name on American shows."

Ben poured another drink, and smiled at Amy. "I have to say I admire you immensely. Confident, attractive. You will go far in life."

"Well, thank you. You're not half bad yourself." They both laughed, and clinked their glasses together. Ben poured more wine into their glasses, and started talking into the late hours on a variety of subjects.

She realized much later that the wine had gone to her head. She was drunk and she knew it. She tried to speak only to find her mouth would not get in sync with her head. Before long she realized she wasn't in the wine cellar anymore.

She tried hard to focus on her surroundings. *I am in bed, that's for sure.* She moved her hands over the top quality sheets. *Am I wearing any clothes? I don't care really.*

She blinked her eyes to find Ben leaning forward, toward her face. He pulled a sheet over her, while Amy gave him her most seductive smile. He kissed her gently on the forehead.

"Why don't you get in beside me?" She tugged his arm, her head spinning.

"You've had too much to drink. Get some rest."

His weight left the bed and he headed for the door.

"Amy, you may wish to inform your mystery man he has a very nice girlfriend." He smiled teasingly and closed the door behind him.

Oh God, he's right! Harry Smith, it's about time you and I got together. The room spinning, her mind racing, she finally drifted into a deep sleep.

Chapter 24

Ben made coffee and sat reading an extensive report from the doctor which Coach had sent early this morning.

Some of this is mind-blowing; the coaches and I will have to be more sensitive to the players. These guys were warriors on the field, but they were all just regular Joes like everyone else outside of football. Many of the players had new wives, or young children and newborn babies all back in the USA. With the season looming, they would not get a chance to visit home for the next few months. *I want my players to have big hearts on that field; last thing I want is my players to have damaged ones.*

He paused at the report on Harry Smith. *Bloody hell, this is extensive.* He read:

Mr. Shannon, please find the following report. As requested, I have tried to keep this in layman's terms for you and your coaches to fully comprehend Harry's condition.

I probably don't need to remind you how uniquely special the position of quarterback really is in the game of football. These individuals literally deal in nanoseconds when making a decision on the play.

They will look off up to five players on each play, read the defense formation all in under three seconds. After studying numerous recorded UT games, I can conclude Harry certainly had that ability. Since the accident, with videos of training camp, my conclusion would be he's at least one second slower in his mental agility, which is not acceptable if one wishes to play this position at top level. I studied all types of defense that were employed in practice and found that blitzing causes him to panic while zone coverage gives him too much time, causing a hesitation in his decision-making. He is over-thinking and receiver routes are breaking down.

My deduction is he does not have the will to think faster, suffering from one of possibly many psychological reactions to his accident. He did suffer a NDE – near death experience – but refused to discuss his experience with me. Many become risk-takers after such an event, thinking they have been given a second chance while others act the opposite. They stay in their comfort zones, worried it could happen again. They become overly careful. Harry is in a comfort zone until something triggers his brain to take charge, think fast, make choices and take risks in a game.

There is no immediate remedy but time. My diagnosis is to keep him up-tempo without forcing him to be the lad he was last year in Texas.

Often survivors of NDE find God, and appreciate nature more than they ever imagined. Birds, trees, plants often place way ahead of day-to-day life issues. Finding that one second will be his choice and could occur at any time, or not at all!

He put down the report with a sigh.

Fuck. This is going to be a tough decision to make.

His thoughts were interrupted by Amy walking gingerly down the stairs. She looked like death warmed over.

"Amy!" Ben's voice halted her in her steps. "Good morning. Would you like a full English or just toast and coffee?"

"Ben, whatever I said last night, I apologize. I had way

too much wine, have a nasty hangover this morning and all I want to do is get home."

Ben poured a coffee and held it out. "Have something to eat and my driver will take you home."

Reluctantly, Amy sighed and followed him. He led her into the custom kitchen and pulled out a stool at a marble-topped island for her. They sat in silence for quite some time. She managed the coffee and a slice of toast. Ben watched the latest stock market news on breakfast TV, giving her the space to wake up. Not everyone was a morning person.

At last, she pushed aside her plate and mug.

"I have to say something before I leave. Ben, I must emphasize: if I said anything inappropriate last night…"

Ben stopped her mid-sentence, switched off the TV with the remote, turning on his barstool to face her. He straddled the stool like he was riding a horse, meeting her eyes forcefully. She gazed back, her eyes wide in surprise, but confident.

"Amy, there is no point in beating around the bush."

Amy avoided his gaze, her face red. She probably thought he was going to scold her about coming on to him last night.

"Harry Smith may be released today," he said simply.

Amy was shocked, her mouth wide open. That obviously wasn't what she expected. "Are you serious?"

"You bet."

"Okay, then." The wheels were turning in her pretty little head. "When will you make it official? I would have to think very hard on my story. I mean, let the fans down gently. Are you sure this is a good move for the Cougars?"

"I said maybe, Amy. I will text you personally later today."

"Okay. Please do, as soon as you've decided. Thanks for having me."

"I'll call my driver for you." Abruptly the conversation was over. He turned the TV back on, his eyes back on the stock market news, but his mind squarely on Harry Smith.

The driver arrived at the door. Amy turned to Ben.

"I will help with Harry, if you decide to keep him. No sweat."

"One of your Plan Bs?"

"I always have a Plan B. You should know that by now."

She shut the door firmly behind her.

Chapter 25

Harry had been informed by one of the coaches that Mr. Shannon would like to see him in his office, immediately. He arrived in reception to see Ben standing at his office door looking somewhat perplexed.

"Come in, Harry." He gestured with his hand in the direction of the spacious office.

"Listen, Harry. The coaches tell me you are not performing well in practice."

"I do all the drills without ever complaining, run a mile without question. What do they mean?"

"I know the effort is there Harry. You're a good team player; I always knew that. Unfortunately, for the position of quarterback we expect far more."

"I've been studying videos with my granddad. The two of us can work it out in time for the season." He rubbed a hand over his face. "Fucking accident. A year off left me rusty, that's all."

"Speaking of the accident, Harry, it's really quite simple. Imagine you had a Harley Davidson bike. You travelled all around Texas on it. Those long roads, the heat, a soft breeze on your face. Think about it, have that vision in your mind for just a few minutes. It's just you and the world.

"Now, out of nowhere a big 18-wheeler hits the bike, you spend weeks in hospital, your legs damaged really bad. A year later, a friend invites you to take his Harley for a ride. You sit on it, engine purring underneath you. What happens, Harry?"

"I don't know Mr. Shannon." Harry didn't like where this conversation was going.

"You get off it! You are scared shitless, body shivering, flashbacks of the accident. That is you right now, Harry. You associate football with your accident. The difference between the bike story and your life is you won't get hurt. There is no pressure from any of us for you to be that QB at UT. Just do your best, son. Will you totally commit to the Cougars, work out this problem and fast?"

"Absolutely. You have my word." Harry shook Ben's hand firmly, trying to show all the confidence he didn't feel.

Ben pulled out his phone and started texting.

"What's that?" Harry asked.

"I'm texting the Cougars girl, Amy Carrington. She'll put this in the Gazette. Now get to practice."

"Yes sir."

Harry smiled at the mention of Amy's name.

Chapter 26

Harry raced from Ben's office to the field to catch up with all the players. He was raring to go; totally motivated and pleased Shannon had complete faith in him.

He had his best practice to date, of that he was totally convinced.

He finally built a relationship with Leroy, the wide receiver. They had just finished 10 yard short passing routines with every ball caught cleanly.

"Hey, Harry let's try a few longer. You do realize I am a wide receiver, broke all kinds of records in college?"

Harry threw a long ball; Leroy was so fast he looked like a cheetah speeding down the sideline. He released the ball with all his might. Reception! Leroy gave a showcase dance, came back to Harry with the ball.

"Cuz, that was like catching a duck! It looked good for the first half of the path, after that it was down and dirty man. If I didn't have good hands, I would never have caught that ball."

Fuck. Long passes had always plagued him. *I can get it there but it never looks pretty.*

He noticed a commotion on the sidelines with Brad and what looked like Amy. *Shit*. He ran over to be in earshot.

"Hey Cougar girl," Brad said with a smirk. "We all loved

that story on the Prince, the washed-up British quarterback. He'll be lucky to survive the training camp. Rumor has it we're bringing in a new backup for me. An American player, just like it should be."

Amy looked puzzled while players congregated around Brad.

"You know my granddad won an Olympic gold medal?"

"Really?" Amy looked surprised. "What was his sport? I'll write something on your background before the season starts."

"Wrestling. He taught me some moves. Come round my place tonight and I'll show you. It works better when we're naked."

The players went into hysterics. Amy didn't look quite so impressed.

Harry was ready to pounce and take his helmet off. Brad would be toast. *I will deck him regardless of the consequences.*

A voice had told him to wait. *Don't do anything to change Ben Shannon's decision today. Wait for Amy to respond.* After all, she was feisty and could handle the likes of Brad Douglas.

"You are a first-class prick. By the way, get your facts right. Take a look on the Gazette website right now. Harry isn't going anywhere."

Good decision, Harry thought. *Amy was awesome, as usual. Man, I like her. When the timing is right I will ask her out. I would have already, only I have to focus on football. A girl like that would be way too much of a distraction!*

He watched her turn and head up the stairs to the exit.

"Fuck it," he murmured, running fast to catch her up. "Excuse me, errmm, just a question really. Have you been to the new nightclub in the city?"

Did Harry imagine the coy smile that played on her full lips?

"No, it just opened last weekend. I hear it's definitely the hip place to be, for sure. Why?"

"Me and some of the players are going to check it out tonight."

"Well I always go out with my girlfriend Liz on a Thursday night to our favorite wine bar … still, we haven't been to a nightclub in weeks. Yeah, maybe it's time to let my hair down, get on the dance floor."

"I hope I bump into you," he said, turning to head for the dressing room.

Man, with her hair down on the dance floor – yeah, I hope I bump into her.

What the hell was he getting himself into? He was supposed to be focusing on football. But something about Amy seemed so right.

Chapter 27

Amy and Liz stood inside the new nightclub in Leeds, admiring the ambience of grandeur. The giant foyer lounge on the ground floor seemed to resemble a tropical paradise. The dance floor was in the far corner, covered all in glass, with people coming in and out of the large doors. When the door was shut, she could only hear a quiet rhythmic sound. Amy smiled, realizing they were playing an old Pitbull classic.

"Okay girl, let's find the Cougars."

There were three bars on offer, situated in three quiet corners.

"Wow, it's warm in here," said Amy, taking off her jacket. "I could have some of this every day instead of the lousy weather we get outdoors in Leeds. Once the Cougar season is over, I am booking a cruise."

"Where to, Amy?" said her friend.

Amy pricked up her ears to a group of men shouting and laughing with a distinct chorus of American accents. "Follow me."

They headed for the bar, where Amy noticed a table full of Cougar players, including Harry. One of the players noticed her and shouted, "It's the reporter!"

"Fucking hell! The paparazzi," shouted another.

One of the American players shouted, "It's about time

the Cougars got some press. We should be the talk of the city."

Amy kept a smile on her face, linked arms with her mate and headed to the bar. They ordered two sparkling wines and sat on the tall bar stools.

I suppose he's right, thought Amy. *I have focused far too much attention on Harry, rather than the team. Still, here he is with the Cougars and looking finer than when we met at Wembley.*

Harry kept his head down – not so much as a peek in her direction. Well, once she showed him what she could do, he would have to pay attention. He couldn't avoid her forever. She'd even traded in her usual pants and flats for a little black dress and four-inch heels. *Okay, two can play at this game.* She could ignore him much longer than he could ignore her.

The lads noticed his careful inattention and started ribbing him. One American tried speaking in a British accent: "You want to shag her, mate?" which sounded ridiculous, while others were hitting him on the shoulders with: "Get over there, mate."

"Shut the fuck up guys! I was just thinking," Harry muttered, low-voiced but not low enough. He shoved the nearest bloke away.

"Yeah, we know what you were thinking."

A few of them raised their glasses in Amy and Liz's direction. "Helloooooooo ladies! Cheers!"

Lads would be lads, and so full of shit when they were out drinking together. They were good at the talk but never the walk. Harry went on giving all his attention to the pint on the table in front of him.

"If I don't make the first move, we'll be here all night,"

she said to her mate. She walked up to the table and grabbed Harry's hand.

"Right then, time for a dance," she said, tugging on his arm. The table went deadly quiet. Harry cast a helpless look at his astonished mates and followed her. His friends erupted into ribald jokes and laughter in their wake.

"Don't worry," she purred. "I'm not here to ask questions."

Harry visibly relaxed, and Amy fought the urge to go back on her word and ask the burning question in everyone's minds: why had Ben Shannon considered sacking him? So far she could only speculate. He seemed committed to the team, but whatever scared Shannon was worrisome.

As they began to dance, though, his interest in her became apparent. He dropped the shy act and met her eyes, devouring her with a fierce hunger. This was starting to become about more than just an inside scoop.

On the dance floor they nailed the first dance mix and when the tempo changed to a slower rhythm, Amy placed her hands on his waist and pulled herself close to him, moving her hips to the song.

"I heard about Yorkshire girls when I was growing up in Cirencester. How forward you are," he whispered in her ear.

"Complaining?" she whispered back.

"Not at all. In fact, I like it," he replied, nuzzling his chin gently into her right shoulder.

She rotated her hips, dancing close between his legs, moving up hard to the beat of the music. Just for a split second, she felt his hardness brush against her. Amy was losing control, her wild side kicking in fast. Her body was aching for him, her nipples erect, her body tingling from head to foot.

"I have some nice wine back at my place if you can pry yourself away from your mates."

Harry seemed taken aback for a moment. He paused for a long time, breathing fast in her ear. Then he chewed her ear lobe, whispering the words she was dying to hear, "Yes please."

They left without passing Harry's table. Amy texted her mate as they slipped out a side door, Harry's hands still on her waist. *You're on your own the rest of tonight!*

Liz texted back: *Have fun! Jealous.*

The ride to her flat was excruciating, being so close to him – the fleeting glances, his hand rubbing her thigh.

By the time they got to the flat, Amy had decided to be cool. She unlocked the building door and spun toward him coyly as they went inside.

This wasn't the guy to emulate some of the popular sex scenes in a movie. He wasn't about to give her what her animal desires yearned for. She eyed him in the elevator, daring him to push her against the wall and kiss her hard with his tongue deep in her mouth. He didn't take the bait, but pulled her gently to him, kissing her tenderly instead.

When they got inside her flat, her heart was pounding with the desire to tear off his clothes and have him tear off hers. In her fantasy he would pick her up, both of them naked with the slightest of ease, carry her to the bedroom and make wild passionate love to her.

No, she knew it would not be like that. She had taken the lead, been the instigator and seducer all night – and with Harry alone for the first time, it would have to be slow.

She poured the wine and they both sat on the sofa, tapping their glasses together in a toast. They talked for what seemed like hours, sharing slow lingering glances and touches.

Amy poured them each a last glass of wine, took a sip and laid her glass on the table. His eyes devoured her, showing how much he fancied her in the new sexy dress. She stood a few feet away from him, smiling softly, head to one side, moving her long hair to fall down one shoulder.

He watched her, hypnotized. "I haven't felt like this in a long time. Not since my accident."

That was surprising. A red-blooded young male like Harry? Amy smiled seductively. "I'll take that as a compliment," she purred.

Slowly and delicately, she put her hands up her dress, dropped her knickers over her hips and walked out of them toward him. His eyes widened. She unzipped his pants and mounted his lap gently, her eyes looking deeply into his. With one deft movement, he was deep inside her.

Warm, pulsating, so deep inside, she was moving slowly, her hips moving like they had to the song in the nightclub when she'd first felt his want. He groaned softly and buried his face in her hair, biting at her neck. His hands grasped around her waist. She'd known how good this would feel from the moment she'd first met Harry. It was all she could do to keep it slow, to savour the feel of him inside.

After minutes of slow rhythmic sexual bliss, the iPod shuffled to a slightly faster song. It was a rap with a powerful throbbing beat. Amy followed the music, her hips rotating harder, gradually becoming faster. She glanced at Harry's face, satisfied and titillated by the look of exquisite heaven on his features.

Her song selections created a perfect crescendo, a slow and gentle pace, now leading up to immense intensity. They both reached climax exactly at the same time, with the ultimate crash of music, and subsided against each other the moment the song came to an end.

They held each other tight in the pulsing silence for a few minutes. Then Amy stood, taking hold of his hand, and pulled him gently into the bedroom. They made love again, only this time she let Harry take the lead. They both fell into a deep sleep in each other's arms.

Sometime in the night, Amy lay wakeful and naked in bed.

Some days are like diamonds while most are like stones. Yesterday – specifically last night – was a 10-karat day.

She looked over at Harry, propping up on her elbow and running her hand gently through his hair. He sighed and smiled in his sleep. It took all of her control not to mount him and wake him slowly, inside her. Make love for the third time, slip into the shower together, make love again. She was hungry for him. He wasn't the only one newly awakened. She hadn't felt this way in at least three years.

She fought to turn away from him and looked at her watch on the nightstand.

"Silly girl," she whispered to herself. *We've only been asleep two hours and we both have work today.* She could always call in sick and get away with it. But Harry? Harry could not miss training today; it was close to the season's opening game.

She lay back on the pillow and thought about how they got here, in her bed, finally together.

Chapter 28

Harry was awake, trying hard to keep his breathing pattern normal. He kept his eyes shut and resisted even the faintest smile on his face.

He had been daydreaming for the last hour about how spectacular last night had been. He recalled their first brief encounter at Wembley more than six months previously. He had been taken aback by Amy's beauty and self-confidence even then, and yet that was only a part of his attraction to her. There was something else so powerful that was difficult to comprehend.

The minute she had sat down at the table that day at Wembley, with a quick glance in his direction while being perfectly professional with Ben Shannon, he'd felt a connection that seemed to develop instantaneously between the two of them. He had wanted her ever since and last night was all about being cool, letting her lead and keeping his overwhelming desires for her in check. Turned out, he hadn't needed to worry. Even now she was awake, and after him again.

I have never had a wakeup call like this!

He responded to her hand under the duvet, stroking him. The full hardness was immediate. Not like him at all first thing in the morning. He felt her slowly move on top of him, gently maneuvering until he was inside her with just a small amount of penetration. Slowly she moved her hips until he was deep – my God, so fucking deep. He heard the groans, that sexy voice she had. "Well aren't we a heavy sleeper?"

"Wow," he said quietly as his big blue eyes popped open in surprise. "I'm not usually a morning person. I need my coffee to wake up. But never mind. This will do." He smiled.

"It'd better do, mate. Did you really just wake up or have you been acting? I can't believe you could have slept through the last ten minutes."

Harry didn't answer, since his mind was focused on the most gorgeous sight he had ever seen. Her skin was a golden brown like coffee: dark roast with a touch of cream. He moved his head from the pillow, leaning up to her face, chewing on her ear lobe, kissing her neck and whispering in her ear. "Be quiet, stop talking."

"I can do that." She pushed him back down to the bed with a sexy smile. He was so ready for her. She quickened her pace until she rode him hard like a horse in full gallop. They both came together, their timing impeccable, and she collapsed on him, her legs wrapped around his waist.

"Whew, that was a nice way to work out. I guess it's training all day for you with the big game coming up in less than two weeks."

"Nice change of pace. Here we are lying naked and you decide to bring up football. You seem to be really into it. Why don't you talk some football, Cougar girl?"

She moved against him as she spoke. "How about 46 defense from the 1985 Chicago Bears? The London Ravens use a similar defense, so be careful with all that blitzing they do. Try a draw play or misdirection, and, of course, the quarterback keeper."

"That would be me." He smiled.

"You wish!" They both laughed.

Harry grabbed a pillow from behind him and threw it at her. She ducked and it sailed over her head.

"What a terrible throw! Overthrowing your receiver. Tut, tut."

"Not exactly an easy throwing position. And let's be realistic: I'm not likely to be this distracted on the field."

Amy pulled away and knelt over him with a playful smile. "First in the shower gets their back washed." She leapt from the bed with a wild laugh.

Harry caught her just before the bathroom door with a diving tackle around the waist. He gave her a quick kiss on the head and with a cheeky grin was in the shower. Amy joined him, her breasts pushed hard against his back, her hand between his legs. *Man, what a girl. I will either be on top of my game at practice or worn out.*

"Hey! The deal was a back-wash and massage. I have a big day at training camp with little time left to beat Brad for that starting position."

"Are you complaining?" She found the soap and poured a huge amount into her cupped hand, then pushed her fingers hard into his shoulders. She put her lust aside in favor of a more practical approach.

"You need to practice your throwing. That pillow was way out of your receiver's reach. I agree you don't need distractions. Move to one side and let me shower, big guy."

Amy showered and made a quick exit, leaving Harry to enjoy a long shower without her.

The water felt good against his skin. In fact, his whole

body was alive, and this was the best he had felt in ages. He noticed Amy had come into view through the steamy shower glass wearing a bath towel tightly around her body, her hair long and wet. *Damn football. Why did I let her get out?*

He turned off the shower, sliding the door open to step into the bathroom naked.

"What were you saying Amy? I couldn't hear you with the shower on."

Amy was lost in thought, staring at him well below his eyeline. "Hey, I have today's storyline."

"Hmm?" Harry grinned, enjoying the ego boost her admiration was giving him.

"Harry Smith of the Leeds Cougars denied sexual advances from yours truly this morning. While I massaged his back and other places, stark naked in the shower, Harry was quoted with the following statement: 'Leave me alone, you nymph! I have less than two weeks to beat out Brad Douglas for the starting QB position!'"

"Now, that would go viral," he laughed.

Chapter 29

Denis Bazan was pacing around his high-rise London office. Every season to date, he'd been relaxed. No worries with the London Ravens. They were miles ahead of any other team in the league. This year, however, they had the new fucking Leeds Cougars to contend with. He had summoned his two coaches to get here immediately, if not sooner.

The two coaches came in to the room; one was a large African-American guy from Alabama that took care of the defense. The other took care of the offense and looked more like a nerd. He was born in California but had lived in England for five years, coaching the Ravens.

"Now we're getting close gents, only two weeks. We start the season in Leeds, shitty Leeds. What are the experts saying?"

"We'll take it again; no problem, boss, with Manchester second and Leeds third."

"That would do nicely. Beat a pair of Northern bastards that need to be kept in their place, with the Ravens firmly on top. What about all the hype with the fucking Leeds Cougars and their dome stadium?"

The defense coach spoke. "We have watched videos of all the teams and there is no doubt we have the best defense in the country. Cougars could have a good offense if the old

Harry Smith showed up in practice. So far, Smith looks like a former shadow of his days in Texas. Their starter Brad Douglas is technically sound but no way could he beat our D."

"Harry Smith? Yeah, I met him at Wembley. He was the first Brit to play QB across the pond."

"Yes," said the offense coach. "He was good, no mistake – until his accident. Don't think his heart is in it these days."

"Now, gentlemen, I've just read the morning paper. This reporter in Leeds – a bit of a good looker, actually – is chattering away about fucking Harry Smith making the team and ready to go. I don't like it!

"Something is telling me the Cougars could cause an upset: one of those fairytale stories I detest. It happens all the time in the FA cup with them giant-killing acts. Look at Bradford City a few years back, in the lowest division beating Arsenal and Aston Villa. I couldn't handle it. If that happened to the Ravens, heads would roll."

He stared at the two coaches. The terror in their eyes reminded him of his old man again. He thought about him often and that would make him miserable, want to kill someone on the spot.

He thought about the only week his Dad was ever happy when he was just a young kid. Chelsea tied the Wembley final. The teams met in the replay and beat them 3-2 in what they say is still one of the best FA cup matches in history. His dad went and got a big tattoo on his lower arm that read *FA Cup Final 1970 Chelsea 3 –Leeds 2.* For the next two weeks, life was good. No beatings for him and his mum. If his beloved Chelsea would have ever lost to an underdog, he could visualize the severity of numerous beatings.

"Right, then. Back to work. And remember – no losses this season, not to anybody, and especially that scum up in Leeds."

Denis was shaking with anger as he dismissed the coaches and sat at his desk. The thought of losing would always drive him insane. He had to call Eric, make sure there would be no upsets, with the Ravens unbeaten as usual.

On second thought, all his top operative would need is a text: *I want you in Leeds this week. Go to the Cougar Dome. Plant bugs in Ben Shannon's office and hack his computer.*

A few seconds later a message came back: *On it, boss.*

Chapter 30

Ben called for a full meeting with coaches and players. Training camp had gone particularly well over the last few weeks. They had the look of a winning team and it was now the right time to boost morale and discuss the game plan for the opening game with the Ravens.

He checked his watch, realizing he was early, full of energy, on edge, ready to start the season. He sat in the leather armchair and mentally rehearsed his plan. Hopefully this was the right strategy to win the British Football League championship in their first season.

As soon as he'd bought the Sheffield team and the Leeds land, he'd called a dear friend on Skype. John was a top NFL scout that had retired two years ago.

"John! How the hell are you? How is the golf game? With all that free time on your hands, you must be playing off scratch."

"Ben, my golf game has improved, but what do you really want? I've never known you to call just to shoot the breeze."

"Would you go to Canada for me?"

John had left the monitor and Ben could hear him laughing in the background. He finally came back, still twitching with laughter. "Scout CFL players and freeze my butt off in Canada?"

"Yes, I'm aware this is a big favor John. I'll owe you big

time. But listen, here's my plan: The BFL players are low-end college drafts that didn't make the cut either on draft day or at training camp. It kinda goes by weight and height for many positions, as you know too well. The NFL has a minimum size and if you're under you have little chance of making it. That translates nicely to playing in Canada with a different set of rules and a wider pitch, allowing quick players to excel. However, the BFL are still playing football with a rugby mentality. They use lots of running plays and big powerful defensive players. You have to stop the running game first and foremost in the UK.

"Here's where I want to change things: we will adopt a West Coast style offense and play like the Patriots. Slot receivers for short pass completions, two tight ends, only one wide receiver used sparingly. Establish the short passing game initially and then hit them with quick running backs. Defense would be tougher. I'd rely on you for your input. What do you think John? Is this doable?"

"Possibly, but how much are you willing to pay for the good ones?"

"The big kicker here is CFL players' average salary is under 100,000 dollars. That is 60,000 pounds – a steal! Tell them it's all negotiable and they get to live in Leeds – the top city in the North of England. It has the lot, John: real ale, fish and chips, lovely forward women."

"Okay, Ben. I get the point. You don't have to be a salesman with me. Long time since I was in England. I'll get up to the frozen North and after I find you your players, you can invite me over to see your magnificent Leeds."

Within a matter of only a few months, John had excelled

in finding Ben a squad of players. His talent at sniffing out a bargain was legendary in the football world. Many players had jumped at the chance of playing in England and for more money than they were currently making. Each time John had sent a message to Ben, he would always finish with, "By the way, I am freezing up here. You owe me big time."

There was a knock at the door, and the head coach poked his head in. At a nod from Ben, coaches and players strolled into the large conference room.

"Good morning! Help yourself to tea or coffee and take a seat. Thank you all for coming and let me say first of all that this is a one-off. As the owner and GM of the Cougars, this will be my only meeting with you, unless there is a special situation. Let's hope that does not occur this season. After this, your head coach and his assistants will have regular player meetings with you. I am hands-on; played free safety at college level and know the game. However, I will not be meddling with the playbook, team selection or any of the day-to-day routines.

"Most of you here are from the Canadian Football League and probably wondering why you were chosen, especially since we don't have a wider field in the UK. For all the offensive players, I hope you are familiar with the New England Patriots."

Ben received groans around the room, smiled and continued. "I did say familiar, not fans. However, they do have a style that will fit perfectly in the BFL. On defense, it's simple: all teams will run the ball 80% to 90% of the game. The RB's are big and strong, often with a leading full back. You play up and make them pass – it's that simple. Eight – or nine – men front-blitzes the QB from the outside, initially giving him no time to pass. Whatever it takes, stop the run!

"Finally let's make one thing perfectly clear: thanks to some free press we are on the map across the country. Yes, we have a British star in our midst that has not played ball for over a year."

He gave Harry a nod and a few players turned to glance at him. "Harry Smith is our backup QB for Brad. Brad will run the offense at all times in the style we have just discussed. If Brad suffers any setbacks or injuries, Harry will take over. At the time, the coaches will change it up to accommodate Harry with some read option plays. They are now in your playbooks.

"I was going to give a speech, deep, like a US president on inaugural day. I could quote Churchill, for example: The problems of victory are more agreeable than the problems of defeat, but they are no less difficult."

Two players nodded. The rest looked glazed.

"I thought so. Gents, this will be short and sweet. I just want to remind you of who you are. By the way, who are you?"

There was a pause around the room.

"Should I ask again?" asked Ben, his voice louder.

"Cougars!" the players shouted.

"Exactly. We are the Cougars, gentlemen. We have our Cougar Dome, our den. We are extremely territorial, proud of our home. Representing this fine animal, this large cat, we are strong, yet with grace, and nothing on this planet can beat us when it comes down to stalking and ambush.

"We don't roar like a lion, wondering why the wife has

not returned with our supper. We are the hunters and our prey is any team that comes in here expecting to beat us. This will never happen. Are you with me?"

The players cheered in agreement.

"Now, gentlemen, do me proud a week Sunday. This is the game, the opener to gauge our season. If we beat the reigning champions on our own turf, we will go all the way and meet them again in the British Bowl final, of that I have absolutely no doubt."

Brad Douglas stood, then turned to the players. "Whose house?" he shouted.

The players responded, "Our house!"

"Who are we?"

"Leeds Cougars!"

"Who are we going to beat?"

"The Ravens!"

They all cheered and left the room. Ben watched them go with a satisfied smile.

Let the season begin.

Chapter 31

Amy squeezed her Mini Cooper into a tight spot in the centre of Leeds, found change for the parking meter and entered the shop. She was on a mission to buy something small for the man who had everything. She had decided it must be a gift related to wine and not too expensive for her tight budget. She realized the day after Ben's housewarming party that she had forgotten to bring a gift.

She picked up decanters, glasses, each time pulling a face once she checked the price tag. Finally she found a wide selection of wine charms that were in her budget. *Well he won't have any of these. He's unlikely to use them, but it's the thought that counts,* she decided. *The only problem now was finding which ones would best suit Ben.* She opted for a set of charms with a golf theme, recalling somewhere in her original research of Ben Shannon that he was or had been a golfer.

She drove her zippy car through the centre of Leeds and out on to the ring road heading for the dome. She arrived at the huge empty car park, stepped out of the car, gazing at the magnificent stadium.

Well girl, what a year. The opening game is just over a week away; Harry will be inside, right now, training hard. She smiled. That chance encounter at Wembley was a life-changer.

She hadn't let go of her goal to be a top professional journalist, the Cougar girl. But really her mind was full of

Harry. She wanted to sit next to him. Her feelings were so strong – the immediate connection to him was something she had never encountered. That had all occurred in the first few minutes of meeting him. Damn! Their first night in bed together had been a long time coming, but worth the wait.

Ben, on the other hand, was like the big brother she'd never had and always wanted. She wanted to spend the rest of her life with Harry and yet she totally loved being in Ben's company.

Okay, girl; let's drop off this gift with Janice. Then you can write a brilliant story on the Cougars in preparation for the big game. Harry wearing his football uniform, throwing the ball, his tight pants. Wow!

She almost ran to the entrance flashing her reporter's badge at the security guard. She made her way up to Ben's office, but found it empty. Even his receptionist's desk was abandoned. But then she saw movement through Ben's office window.

"Ben are you in there? Janice must be on a tea break. Just have something to leave for you."

She opened the door, revealing a stranger, dressed all in black and wearing leather gloves. Their eyes met. Amy froze.

The intruder was like greased lightning, at the door in less than a second, hitting her square in the jaw with a right hook.

She staggered around the office. Her shopping bag flew in the air. The man hit her again on the back of the head and she was falling down, hitting the desk hard on the side of her head. Finally she lay motionless on the wooden floor.

She soon regained consciousness, feeling a leather-gloved hand over her mouth. "Such a shame it's not possible to sneak you out, back to my pad in Manchester for some fun," she heard him whisper. The room was going dark, stars sparkling. From the mists she heard a shout from the office entrance. The creepy guy released his hand from her mouth and moved towards the computer. Amy thought it was Ben's voice. She forced a smile as her eyes became heavy, drifting back into a dark place.

Chapter 32

"What the fuck?" Ben spotted a figure moving across his office window. The office was positioned behind the Cougar end zone where the players were practising a goal line defense play. The shadowy figure wasn't right. No one should be in there.

He started moving, sprinting across the field, shouting "Some guy is in my office!" The players stopped their drills and watched him go.

Ben puffed up the stairs and froze at the door. In his office, a strange man stood, dressed in dark clothes and leather gloves. He stood over someone, but not until he bent over her and put a hand over her mouth did Ben recognize Amy Carrington.

"Hey!" he shouted, moving toward the intruder.

The man panicked, grabbed something from Ben's computer and charged the office door. Ben tackled him down to the ground, with a hit reminiscent of his college days playing free safety. The intruder kicked him hard in the balls, providing him a second to slip from Ben's grasp and out of the door. Ben was up and staggering, dashing for the phone. "Security, we have an intruder leaving my office!"

He knelt down at Amy's side, taking in the blood trickling from her head, the bluish tinge of her lips. He put two fingers to her carotid, but found no pulse.

Harry came in with some of the players behind him. When he saw Amy, he went into a total frenzy. "Amy, no!" Pushing off his fellow players, he fought to Ben's side and went down on his knees.

"Calm down, Harry." Ben took a breath. "Have you ever done CPR training?"

"Yes. I took a class in college."

Harry sprang into action, giving orders.

"Go to her head. Raise her chin to open her airway." Ben did, watching Harry go to work. He pushed on her chest in a rhythmic fashion, counting to five, to ten, to fifteen. Then he pushed Ben aside and gave her the kiss of life. Her face was still blue, her pulse faint.

Ben called 999 and explained while Harry continued with his CPR maneuver. He put the phone on speaker so Harry could hear the instructions, then got down and took over chest compressions while Harry breathed. They were a team, with Amy's life in their hands.

In between breaths, Ben could hear Harry murmuring to Amy.

"How long before you're here?" Ben shouted into the phone.

"We are pulling up at the stadium right now."

Harry checked her pulse again, looked at Ben with haunted eyes, shook his head. "I won't lose Amy. No fucking way."

Ben felt the same.

Part 3

Chapter 33

Amy was in the hospital.

A tall skinny man with sharp piercing eyes and a beard leaned over her bed, staring at her. She could not move or shout; she was pinned to the bed by an unknown force. He had a toolbox laid on the bed by her feet. He took out a hammer and large screwdriver which he placed on her right breast. The hammer came down on her, the tool piercing through her body. She screamed.

Two nurses ran to her side holding her hands.

"Amy, you had a bad dream."

Nightmare, more like it. The same one I've had for years. She started to sob. She flashed back to the black leather glove hitting her face so hard, falling down so fast, white lights flashing all around her. How could that have happened in Ben's office?

She never expected a violent attack. She was incredibly street-smart – had been ever since the day she'd picked up a book her dad was reading. The Yorkshire Ripper: A True Story. She'd noted it was from the early eighties.

This was for real and in her backyard. Not in her time, thank God, but her mum and dad would have been teenagers at that time. The book was explicit with lots of photographs of the victims. She had checked the story on Google and could not believe what she read. Thirteen women murdered, seven more attempted murders. A modern-day Jack the Ripper, roaming the streets at night on the prowl in Bradford and her beloved city of Leeds.

She found a site showing many of the obituaries in the paper and it completely freaked her out. Imagine that happening to your daughter and reading about in the bloody paper.

"I thought obituaries were for old people," she had said to her dad.

"Unfortunately not always." He'd had tears in his eyes.

"You must have been right there when this was going on, Dad. In Leeds? No, wait a minute. You were at Bradford University in 1980, right?"

Her dad had nodded. "I bought the book to remind me of someone, one of his victims."

"No way! You've never mentioned this before." Amy had listened in horrified fascination.

"It was all so surreal back then. We never expected he would be living on our doorstep. Hell, his wife was from the same tiny village as one of our cousins. I didn't know the girl well but had been to some of the same parties. We said hello, how are you, that kind of thing. You just never expect something so evil to be so close to people you know. Make sure you are always vigilant, especially when you start going out with your mates drinking."

"I will, Dad." She had given him a big hug.

She'd vowed to have eyes in the back of her head and she would never look at that book or an obituary section again, not ever.

Amy heard a voice and forced her eyes to open. The

nightmare was gone, her negative thoughts dispelled at least for now.

"How are you?" asked Harry.

"Thank God you're here. I just had a nasty dream."

He was at her side in an instant, his arms around her in a crushing hug.

"Hey, thanks for saving me. I heard you and Ben were amazing."

"We worked together. Thank God I had attended a class on CPR. Ben was really shaken by the whole incident."

"What about you?"

"I had no time to think, my instincts just took over." He fought back the tears that were building up, his body began to shake. "Amy, I kept it together until the paramedics came and after that I was a total mess."

"I saw you there with me, right by my side, making me feel comfortable."

Harry looked at her, questioning.

"Oh, it's too complicated to describe right now."

"You mean out-of-body-experience?"

She nodded.

"We can compare notes sometime in the future."

"You had one too with your coma?"

"Yep and it was really weird. Now, can I have another hug?"

"No, you're too rough," she said smiling. "Do we have any idea who almost killed me? Why was he in Ben Shannon's office? Why…"

"Hold on Amy, calm down. No is the answer, they don't have a single lead at this point. The police are all over the dome, checking for clues, DNA evidence. It seems the intruder was a professional, wore gloves."

The black glove reappeared in her mind. She shuddered. "What the hell could he have been doing in Ben's office?"

"Let's change the subject, okay?"

"Okay then. Tell me about the Cougars and the game on Sunday. I'll have to start writing my column today."

"Hang on, Amy. You need some rest. You almost died."

"Okay, but only today. Then I need to be out of here."

"No you do not! We need our Cougar girl rested and fresh," came a Yorkshire/Texan hybrid voice from the door.

"My other hero! Thanks for saving me. Harry was just explaining those CPR maneuvers you both performed on me."

Ben placed two large bouquets of flowers on the bed.

"I'll have the nurses put these in a vase for you."

"Ben, I was asking Harry why someone would be sneaking around your office."

"Too early to draw any conclusions, however, we believe it was one of my business competitors, looking for files on a big deal we're working on back in Texas." Something about the way he shied away from her gave her the feeling he lied. "Now, enough of the questions and get some rest."

He headed for the door, then paused, "I do have just one question for you. Why did you come by my office on a Friday morning? You know I'm always down on the field when we have practice."

"I brought you a housewarming gift. I forgot to bring one to the party."

Ben smiled. "That was sweet of you. The office has been

cordoned off until later today. I haven't seen it yet. Well, I need to get back to the Cougar Dome. Big weekend coming up."

"Yep," said Harry, "I'll be there for practice."

Ben came back to the bed and picked up one of the bouquets. "Just going to pop in and cheer Janice up."

"Oh my God," said Amy. "How is Janice? I heard she is down the corridor."

"She'll be fine. Just has a mild concussion. I'll see you both later."

Ben closed the door after him.

"A housewarming party?" asked Harry.

"Yeah. It was a chance to see the Shannon mansion and mingle with some of the Cougar sponsors. Ben was showing me his wine collection and you know how much I love wine."

"I do. I'm glad you're okay, Amy. Now, time for some rest. I'll come back tonight." He gave her a big hug and headed out of the ward to the elevator.

Amy thought it was kind of cute the way Harry got suspicious about Ben's housewarming party. She'd have to try a little harder to make sure he knew she wasn't going anywhere.

Chapter 34

Harry returned that evening as promised, pleased to see Amy already looking so much better than the morning.

"Hey, Harry! My parents just left. They brought me my Mac. God, this place is so boring. Tell me about practice. What's the word in the Cougar camp? Give me some scoop, dude! Will you or Brad be starting?"

"I feel like I'm being interviewed at random." He laughed.

"Shut up and get on with it."

"The city is pumped for the game and they estimate a good crowd, bearing in mind it's the other football game on display. The team looks really good. Brad's the starting QB. The ex-CFL players are really quick and better than most in the BFL."

"Will we win?" asked Amy.

"We should at home, but it is the reigning champions. The Ravens have an awesome defense."

"Why Brad, over you?"

Harry shrugged. "He knows the system, the playbook inside out. Right now he's the better choice. I'll be on the bench and ready if anything should happen to Brad. The Cougar offense is set up better for a pocket QB rather than my read option style. It's nothing like Texas. But I'll get used to it."

"Are you feeling okay, I mean is your passion for the game back?"

"I feel better but still weird; I can't put my finger on it. I'm not as good as my days in Texas, that's for sure. I'm in better shape physically thanks to the tough training camp. Mentally, I don't seem quite as sharp.

"But enough about me! I asked the nurse when I came in about your status. It seems they want to keep you in for quite some time for observation. I wish you could have made the game on Sunday."

"Harry Smith, I will be at the game. No bloody way will I miss the game! I am coming – get that through your thick Southern skull." She grinned.

"Okay," he surrendered, "but if you do manage to escape, please do me one favor."

"Name it."

"Let G Pops sit next to you in the press section. I told him not to buy a ticket and that you would arrange a press box seat for him. Thing is, after the interview, he likes you a lot and his knowledge of the game will help you. You might have a post reaction or something and need his help for the report."

She pondered for a long moment, made him think she was going to say no, then smiled. "It's a deal. Now get lost while I figure out a plan to get out of here in time for Sunday."

Chapter 35

Ben woke early on Sunday, made coffee and checked his messages on the monitor. 24,000 tickets sold for the game. Not bad.

The last message was from Andy. *Hey boss, a nice surprise for the opener. I convinced the band playing at half-time to do a publicity stunt. Their first single from their new album is not due out for three more weeks. They are going to play it today. Check the Twitter account link I've included below.*

Ben clicked on the account link: 4.5 million followers were tweeting about the single and asking how to get tickets to the game.

Ben didn't care how he got bums on seats in the early stages. Once they saw American football at this level, flying the Yorkshire flag, his goal of 40,000 would be easy.

He messaged Andy back. *Nice one Andy. That was beyond the call of duty.*

Ben entered the owner's box. The Ravens' management was in an adjoining private box, which Ben had specifically requested when building the dome.

He'd said, "I want everybody to feel welcome at the Cougar Dome – even our opponents."

Denis was already there, getting the lay of the land. He caught Ben watching him, gave him a quick two-finger fuck-off and smiled with a fake wave.

I will deal with you in the near future, Ben thought, smiling back with a nod.

The crowd looked to be over 35,000. Ben's only disappointment was the lack of Cougar regalia worn by the fans.

I'll have our PR department do a sales drive next week. Best we win today and it will be far easier.

Chapter 36

Amy had been given the all-clear the night before, on the understanding she stayed with her parents for seven days.

"No problem," she'd told the doctor. *Some of Mum's Italian cooking and dad's wine – it's a deal.*

She had sent a text to Ben asking for a third seat in the press box. Dad would have to come.

They arrived at the stadium in the thick of a huge crowd. They drove through tailgate parties with hotdogs and beers to find a parking spot, and Amy noticed many fans were young, but wearing no Cougar colours. They were probably only here for the band playing at half-time. She had read all the tweets last night and early this morning.

Excitement was building as they entered the stadium. Amy realized this was the first time she'd been here since the attack last Friday.

Girl, it's in the past. Move on. She turned her attention to the spectacle in front of her. She had only seen the dome almost empty, with just forty or so players on the field, much of the surroundings still a work in progress.

"Wow!" She switched on her Canon camera. "I need some shots for my blog." She smiled at Paul and her dad.

The Cougar Dome was designed around the habitat of the North American cougar. The seating was arranged to have the effect of a mountain range – the large field intended to be a lake, although it was green rather than blue. However, the blue and gold of the team was a perfect blend, highlighted in both end zones.

The giant screen displayed footage of cougars with messages of thanks for all attending the game today. The caption read, *A portion of your ticket fee has gone to the conservation of these marvelous creatures*. Amy knew people still hunted them, although not in the heavy numbers that had occurred in the last millennium.

Another screen showed all the special guests at the stadium today: actors, sports personalities and politicians. As they were about to take their seats, her dad said, "No way!" and pointed at the screen.

She almost fainted. "Where did they get a picture of me?" she yelled. The message read, *Amy Carrington, you gave us all a scare. Glad you made it today.* "Flaming hell!"

"You have superstar status! You deserve it." Her dad gave her a big hug. "Now, just be a little more careful from now on."

"I always am, Dad. Friday was a one-off."

Chapter 37

Harry watched the Ravens methodically take the ball down the field with a long ten-minute drive, finally running in a touchdown. Brad came on to answer them but as half-time loomed, the Ravens were in complete control. Brad had no effect and now Harry knew why they had stayed unbeaten for all these years. Their defense was solid, with fast blitzing stunts that kept Brad totally off balance.

The half-time entertainment should take their minds off the game for a while, but this looks grim. They should give me a shot, thought Harry.

The Ravens added a touchdown in the third quarter to make the score 21-7 in their favor. Harry spotted Ben Shannon heading towards the sideline. He inched closer to the coaches. With his helmet off, he could overhear their conversation. Seemed like the owner was demanding he should be in the game. The bloody coaches were pleading their case to give Brad more time. *Morons*, he thought. He heard Ben raise his voice. "Coach, we need to give Harry a try-out."

"Just thinking the same, Mr. Shannon. I will have him on in the fourth quarter."

Harry smiled. *So the owner does have some faith in me.*

Meanwhile, the Ravens had complete control of the game. The fourth quarter arrived and Harry ran to the coach.

"Coach Greaves, let me have a go. We can still win this game."

"Okay son, get on there."

Harry walked onto the field to a huge roar from the crowd, taking a deep breath and reviewing the playbook in his mind. The Ravens seemed to stay in their same defense without a spy. A spy was employed by a defense whenever they were up against a fast quarterback that liked to run the ball himself. Harry decided on a play meant to be their downfall. He would use the read option play, running the ball with fake pump passes and misdirection running plays.

Harry came into the huddle, the players around him, panting, their heads down looking totally defeated, hoping Harry would provide a spark in the game. "Okay, read option, just follow my count and no going offside. They are just a team we have to beat, forget they are the Ravens."

He bent down behind the centre, his eyes reading the defense. The whole dome was quiet with all noise coming from the defense players; their breathing was loud, their eyes focused on one player – him.

"Hey, it's the wimpy English boy with the reporter girlfriend. I had her last night and she thanked me for being the first real man she had in years."

Harry paid no attention; he was far more concerned that one of his linemen would be rattled by the comment. Linemen always protected their QB.

"Ohio 42 on two, hut, hut."

Harry ran round the right side with two defensive players reading the play running laterally at full speed, heading straight for him.

Block one of them and I can handle the other, he hoped in his mind. A Cougar slot receiver put a perfect block on the first player. Harry faked his left shoulder to look like he was coming back in. The player dived, missed and Harry was running for the end zone.

Touchdown!

Harry scored in similar fashion on their next drive before the Ravens overcame their pride, reluctantly admitting they would have to change their format. They used two spotters, giving Harry no chance of running the ball himself. With two minutes left in the game, the score was now tied at 21-21. Harry made a play upfield, only to be stopped twice in a row by the Ravens' adapted defense. The game was now in a deadlock with both teams' defense playing stellar football.

On what could have been the last drive of the game before heading for overtime, Harry stayed more in the pocket, throwing a series of short passes to advance the ball to the Ravens' 25-yard line. Harry gave everything he had. He took the ball well inside the Ravens' half, resulting in a 42-yard field goal attempt to win the game.

The Cougars' coach took a final timeout with three seconds on the clock. The crowd went into a deadly silence, chewing their fingernails in anticipation. This was a long kick under pressure. This was something British fans knew well: kicking the ball. Billy Marriot from Sydney, Australia, the Cougars' kicker, had one hell of a foot and no problem with distance. However, his accuracy was always in doubt.

The ball went sailing high. The air was still in the dome, not a breath of wind. Harry could see it was slightly off line, nearer now with the ball inches from the upright. He held his breath. The ball hit the left upright with a clank, bouncing through for a field goal. Cougars won it 24-21.

The crowd erupted with cheers. Harry was over the moon, running to the fans in the Cougars' end zone. They began a chorus of, "We love you Cougars, we do!"

Harry stood there, in the moment; the other players now joining him. Finally he ran to the sideline to greet Ben Shannon with a high five.

"What a comeback, Harry! Where did that come from?"

"I don't know, boss. Something just seemed to click."

Chapter 38

Harry showered quickly in the dressing room, changing into jeans and a sweatshirt at the speed of light. He literally raced for the doors while some players were shouting, "Give the Cougar girl a kiss from me."

He jumped in the Mini Cooper parked at the main gate. "What did you think about that?"

"Harry, you were brilliant!" Amy greeted him with a kiss. "I'm already working on the story."

"Was G Pops any help? I'll bet he's over the moon. I'll text him right now."

"He was ecstatic. He helped me a lot. His knowledge of the game is far more extensive than I could have imagined. He said, 'That final fifteen minutes you just witnessed was the Harry Smith that played for UT last year.'"

"Can I read what you have so far?"

She nodded, still deep in thought and handed him her laptop.

Harry Smith – Leeds Cougar's Comeback Kid!

The Cougars opened the season at the amazing Cougar Dome with a classic come-from-behind win on Sunday. The London Ravens dominated most of the game with their renowned championship-winning defense. Brad Douglas, the Cougars' starting QB, could not get into rhythm in the face of a bombardment of blitzing by the Ravens' defense. With the Ravens on top 21-7 and only fifteen minutes to go, the Cougars brought on Harry Smith to replace Brad Douglas in the quarterback position. Smith was unstoppable with ten consecutive pass completions, 100 yards rushing and two touchdowns. Billy Marriott kicked the winning field goal with the last play of the game. This is the first loss for the Ravens in over three seasons.

Harry Smith has already been dubbed Supersub on all the social networking channels, being compared to England's soccer legends David Fairclough and Jermaine Defoe.

The next Cougars game will be this Sunday at Bristol. Who should be the starting quarterback? Tweet me @cougargirlthegazette

"Wow! I like that," Harry smiled. "I think all you've forgotten to mention is that this Comeback Kid is the best-looking, super-fine QB in the BFL."

"I was going tell him in person in, oh, about ten minutes, when we go to bed." She smiled wickedly.

"Amy, you are so smart."

Chapter 39

Ben was in the office early checking emails and messages from Janice. He realized that, for the first time in weeks, this would be a relatively quiet day by his standards. He checked the weather forecast, which revealed a sunny day with a high of 18 degrees.

"I do believe it's time to have a day off," he said to himself. Well, not a day off work. However, it was a break from the Cougar Dome, and lunch at his favorite pub and restaurant in England. Janice wouldn't be in for an hour, leaving Ben to organize his day trip. He sent a text to his contact to make sure he would be available for the entire day, receiving a message back two minutes later: *Love to see you Mr. Shannon, I will book your favorite table for lunch.*

Next he thought about calling his driver to bring round the stretch limo, deciding against it at the last second. *I will never relax sitting in the back of that thing; instead I will be on the phone working. I haven't taken out my new Bentley on a long run and the A1 does have some stretches without those dreaded cameras. Maybe I could touch 150 mph, if only for a few seconds.*

He opened the car door, sat in the leather seat and fired up the engine. *Great decision Ben, now let's get on the motorway and see what she's got.*

Once on the motorway, the car purred along in reasonably light traffic for this time of day, and once on the

A1 it would be a breeze. He was looking forward to meeting Raymond, his genie, who he was sure would find a solution to the big problem: the asshole, Denis Bazan.

He entered the ramp to the A1, saw a gap in the traffic, looked down at the gear shift. Back in Texas it was all automatic gears and driving was a tad boring. *Let's see what you've got.* He shifted down into second, the engine roared, he accelerated through the gears, and within ten seconds he was close to 120. *It's about time I had some fun!*

The exit for Stamford appeared and after what seemed like only an hour he was in the town, parking by Raymond's office. He really liked this town and thought it would be a nice place to retire, although he hoped that was many years away. What would he do without work, except get in a few more rounds of golf?

Ben walked in the office to find Raymond sliding on a chair from one giant monitor to the next. He looked up and grinned in surprise.

"Ben Shannon in the flesh! It's been a few years since you've been here in person."

"I know. Normally I would have used our usual video conferencing. However, I felt like a day away from the office and this problem needs the two of us. It is rather personal."

"Ben, whatever you need, name it."

"I need some dirt to use as leverage on Denis Bazan. I know that bastard was behind the intruder at my office. Amy would just be considered collateral damage to him."

"Bazan has a ton of dirt, but it's totally public, Mr. Shannon. He is without doubt one of the most evil human beings in England and quite unique, being one of the top villains in London who can still say he's British. However, he has bought a lot of powerful connections over the years, all in the right places. My dossier I had complied for you last year was quite extensive."

"I know, and thanks, however, I need leverage. Something dark, a secret. I just need to make him realize I have a card to play at any given time. Would you keep looking? For your usual fee, of course, but if you find something I can use I will triple it!"

"Ben, it would be my pleasure to find something juicy on Denis Bazan."

"Why on earth would he be such an idiot, be so obsessive with the Ravens? He has power, money. I could see this if the two of us were involved in a business deal."

"His file shows that growing up he could never excel at sports. His dad was a nasty piece of work. Pushed him hard to be a soccer player. He had two left feet, and the other kids would laugh and bully him on sports days. I would assume the Ravens are his way of being successful in sports; make him feel like a man, one of the boys."

Raymond had already worked on Bazan almost a year ago, compiling a dossier for Ben which had gone back to his family roots in the Basque region of Spain. This was just a dossier to show his client what he would be up against. Checking, probing, and finding every last detail on his personality traits, strengths and weaknesses.

Always know your opponents! That was Ben's philosophy.

Ben watched Raymond go to work, pulling up files at the speed of light, sliding back and forth in his chair to four different computers.

"What are you thinking?"

"I'm finding newspaper articles and photographs over the last twenty years that would involve Bazan. This would be about the time that evil bastard gained notoriety around the UK."

He had been summoned to appear for questioning on many occasions. Charged three times, but nothing ever stuck. If anybody in the government was protecting him, being of assistance in the growth of his empire, it would be a council man or possibly a junior MP.

Reading the entire dossier again, Ben had a gut feeling he would turn up something by focusing on his rise to fame and who would have been there in government around the same time.

He watched Raymond find a list of current officials, setting the filters to cross-match any with Bazan. One name was highlighted several times in current articles, and after he had modified the search to go back twenty years, he had a name! Sir Geoffrey Davenport, top cabinet minister.

"Oh shit," Ben murmured.

Raymond scrolled down the many articles looking at ones from twenty years ago. The first was a landslide win for Davenport, where he had become a newly elected MP.

A few months later, they found a publication featuring a photograph of Davenport and Bazan – all smiles, shaking hands. Denis Bazan had just been awarded the contract on a huge piece of land to build a new housing development, shopping arcades and a park. Raymond now pulled up an original plan that had been all over the papers.

Look at that: paradise in a dingy part of London. That is now the home of the London Ravens along with all the skyscraper offices and hotels. Yet no housing or parks. Bazan, you are a true bastard.

What seemed more curious were the pictures of Denis Bazan and Davenport's wife at various charity functions, which he found further down the screen. It seemed after the land deal, they appeared together at such functions on a monthly basis. Raymond's right hand slid across the monitor, touching the various applications and files, dragging them across the screen at such speed and grace.

He paused, studied each charity event picture, touched on the enlargement function key. Denis had his right hand around her waist; hers around his.

"Their fingers have pressure on each other – like more than just friends," said Ben.

Raymond zoomed in on their eyes.

"I know for a fact these two had sex not long before the pictures were taken." Raymond nodded in agreement.

"Right, let's have lunch at the George and I'll leave this with you. Daily updates as usual?"

"Of course, Ben."

Chapter 40

Ben got in the office early the next morning after his jaunt to Stamford. He felt refreshed and ready for the day ahead.

He read the *Gazette* online. *I will have words with Amy Carrington. But first, Denis Bazan.*

Raymond appeared on the screen a few seconds after Ben touched connect on his monitor. Raymond relayed all of his findings he had been working on since Ben had left yesterday.

"A sex scandal with a top official's wife is not that big of a deal these days," Ben mused. "We see it in the paper on a daily basis. They're probably still together for political reasons. It would be a good card to play if I needed help with the British government, but all I want is Bazan out of my life."

"Ben, how long have you known me? I have something far more interesting. Once you and I had checked all the dates – the land deal, charity events, what have you – I discovered that nine months later, the Davenports had a baby girl. You must have seen Penny Davenport in the news: sailing, mountaineering, tennis, currently attending a top private school in Wales."

"Damn. You see a connection to Bazan?"

"Her eyes, Ben. They are so like all the pictures I sent last year. Remember I went way back on his father's side to the Basque region of Spain?"

"What are you saying, Raymond, for Christ's sake? Penny Davenport is Bazan's daughter?"

"We need a sample from Penny Davenport and Bazan for DNA."

"How the hell will you do that?"

"I have my methods. Do I have the go-ahead?"

Ben thought for a minute. Then he remembered the intruder Bazan had almost certainly sent to steal his files, the one who'd almost killed Amy. "Do what you have to."

That brought him to his next unpleasant task. He called Amy on her mobile.

"Good morning. Amy Carrington speaking."

"What the hell are you doing? I was going to call you earlier on the Comeback Kid story, just to let you know I was very disappointed. And now just to make matters worse, I've just discovered your stunt on Twitter."

"What the heck are you talking about Ben? Would you please change that tone of voice with me?"

The last thing his ego needed was for that upstart girl to tell him he needed to be more professional. But he took a deep breath all the same. "Okay, it *was* a nice comeback. I'll give you that. And yet, if I am not mistaken, American football is a team sport. This was all about your darling Harry Smith. Bad enough I have to read a slew of Cougar fans advising me on who should start on Sunday."

"Flaming hell! I'm just doing my job. I thought involving the fans, firing them up, would be good for the Cougars."

"Yet, Amy, you knew the answer. Of course they would all vote for Harry. But what the fans want, what you want, is not necessarily what the team needs. You've let me down. I had assumed incorrectly that you knew not to mix business with pleasure. Amy, why not focus on the Cougar season without any distractions. After all, we are only talking a few months."

The phone was quiet. Ben thought he heard the whisper, "Bite me." Just like Amy. She could be outspoken at times, a sure firecracker with potential. However, this all had to stop.

"Would you please try to report on the whole team, without any favoritism to any one individual? The article was bad enough, but the Twitter question is far more serious. I don't need my coaches swayed by fan pressure when making their team selection, on any given Sunday."

"Thanks for making me feel like crap. Are we done?"

"Yes."

The phone went dead.

That went well, thought Ben.

Chapter 41

She had stepped over the line. *Of course, flipping Ben Shannon was right as always.* She fumed, wondering how to patch things up.

I have let Harry distract me from my job, even if the game report was factual. Damn, it's just been so long. In fact, I've never felt this way about a guy.

The Twitter idea was stupid and would force the coaches into starting Harry, which was probably not a part of the picture.

I want both guys in my life for totally different reasons. I need Ben for my career and I do find him fascinating, intelligent. He makes me feel like a woman with some brains. Harry makes me feel my age, alive, sexy and desirable, and I have this strong feeling he's the one for me. Okay, time for Harry to meet my family, get to know the whole package and not just my fabulous body.

She sent Harry a message: *Come for dinner tonight at my parents'. 7.30. xxxx*

Chapter 42

Harry showed up at precisely 7:30, bringing a wine for dinner. Amy inspected the label and made a fake smile.

"Nice one. We'll have that with the meal."

I bet the wine is shit, thought Harry.

Amy went to the fridge, pulled out a beer for Harry.

"Peroni?" It was his turn to be skeptical.

"An Italian beer, since we are all Italian tonight," she said, matter of fact. "Let's move to the living room. Mum doesn't like a congregation in the kitchen. Mum, this is Harry, I forgot he's only met Dad."

"We'll talk at dinner," she said to Harry with a smile while tending to the cooking.

Harry smiled back, admiring Amy's mum. *She is a very attractive lady even in a hot kitchen wearing an apron. You always have to look at the Mum to visualize what your girlfriend might look like twenty years later. Alright here*, he thought.

Amy led Harry into the living room, where her dad was watching TV. She picked up a pillow and threw it at him. "Dad, stop watching football, we have a guest."

Harry smiled as Mr. Carrington rose, shaking his hand firmly.

"What game is that you're watching?" Harry inquired as they sat down.

"It's a Super Bowl game between the Steelers and Cowboys. Thanks to this channel I've begun to get the basics of the game. Now, thanks to my daughter, I can follow it far easier."

"Pittsburg," Harry said with a huge moan.

"You don't like the Steelers with Terry Bradshaw?"

"Not really, they're in the same division as the Patriots." Harry watched Bradshaw underneath the center, dropping back and firing a long ball headed for the receiver.

Harry stared at the screen, totally oblivious to any conversation. The long ball had always eluded him. Bradshaw had a strange technique. He recalled reading a story on it, checked it out on YouTube. Almost all QB's use the laces when holding the ball. Bradshaw would place his index finger on the football's point, spreading the rest of the fingers forward. He had tried this technique many times, but only managed to make the ball wobble even more.

"Hey you! Never mind football. Time for dinner." Amy squeezed his shoulder.

The men stood and came to the table. Harry looked at the big bowl of spaghetti, fresh bread, a sauce that smelled divine.

"You sit here," said Amy's mum, pulling out the chair for him.

Harry tucked in. The meal was so incredible he hardly said a word, just made polite nods when he felt it was the right time.

"Seems like Harry likes your cooking, Mum." Amy smiled across the table at him.

"Mrs. Carrington, what was that?" he asked as he put down his fork and leaned back, stuffed. "I've had spaghetti bolognese many times but this was far nicer."

"Grazie, Harry. It would never be the traditional bolognese, since that is from the North of Italy. I was born near Naples. The dish is a mixture of both Italian regions with some British influence."

"You mean the bacon?"

"Yes. Have you ever been to Italy?"

"Yes, Lake Garda. It was amazing."

"You have never been to the South, no?"

"I want to, especially now after this meal."

"You must visit the South of Italy. It is far nicer, and the people are much friendlier. We, too, have a North-South rivalry, like England. I am very concerned, actually, that Amy is dating a Southerner."

The room went quiet. Amy's mum finally burst into laughter, gave him a hug and vanished into the kitchen without another word.

"Now I know where Amy gets her dry sense of humour," Harry said, looking in Amy's direction.

Amy's father left to help in the kitchen while Harry sat with Amy, still raving about the dinner, a glass of Chianti in hand, which was a first.

"This is strange, sitting in your parents' house. Can we sneak in a kiss or two while they're in the kitchen?"

Amy leaned over, kissing him hard on the lips. They hugged for some time until Harry studied the bruises on her face and neck.

"Are you doing okay, I mean, how is the bruising?"

"I'm surviving. I'm going to the hospital in the morning. If I get the all-clear, it will mean moving back into my flat."

"You mean no more of your mum's cooking?"

"Hey I can cook, asshole," she said while they both laughed.

"Not to change the subject, but I hear you were in trouble today on the Twitter messages. I hardly use mine and today I received a ton saying they hoped I would start on Sunday."

"What do you think?"

"Bloody right I should. Thing is, in football, it takes more than one lousy game for the coaches to change QBs. Some teams stay with the starter through thick and thin, which I think is so daft. Have you had any heat from the Cougars?"

"I got a right bollocking from Ben Shannon today."

"What the heck is he spouting about this time?"

"My story was too biased towards someone I seem to fancy far too much." She glanced down at her wine glass, twirling the stem.

"A wise choice in men – just like the wine you pick. You are too bloody influenced by him. Tell him to take a hike."

"Do I detect a tad of jealousy?"

Harry was getting a buzz from the wine. He preferred to stick with beer and now his emotions were reaching the surface, and his brain was becoming fuzzy.

"Yeah, maybe I am jealous. So what is Mr. Bloody Shannon asking you to do?"

"He suggested we both cool our relationship during the season and take it up again after we win the championship. He did point out it's a short season and would be all finished by the start of autumn."

"The whole summer, practically!" he interrupted. "Summer in England is the only time to have fun. The bloody weather drives us all indoors most of the time, sitting watching telly."

"Hey, you! We won't be watching telly on a dreary day. I have far better plans." She leaned over to kiss him.

Harry edged away from her. "Why invite me to meet your wonderful parents if we're going to cool it?"

"To show you what's in the future. Have some patience, grasshopper."

"Why now? What has happened recently I don't know about? Or is it the attack?"

"Look, I have a fantastic career opportunity, while you are on your way back to the good old days, playing football, kicking some butt."

Harry got up, found his jacket and stopped momentarily at the front door.

"I just got it. This smells of Ben-bloody-Shannon. Was it really a bollocking?"

"Hey, I don't lie to you! And stop getting jealous over Ben. He's old enough to be my dad for goodness sake."

"Filthy rich, good-looking – loads of girls go for the older guy."

"I only want to be with you, except I need to focus on the Cougars' season. My career will be judged by my writing in the next two months. I can't afford to be distracted. And neither can you. Why don't you focus on beating Brad for the starting position? That way I can write amazing reports on my guy all the time. I did just make them all wonder who should be the starter now, didn't I?"

Harry stood quietly for a few minutes, his emotions rising. "Your guy is the one and only QB, the guy that won it all in Texas. Have you ever considered getting to know me for who I am? I've changed since the accident, my whole personality. Sometimes I go into dark moods for no apparent reason. You, Ben and G Pops – all you bloody talk about is football. 'When is Harry going to be back to his best like the old days?' Bollocks to the lot of you! And you do have a thing with Ben Shannon. A housewarming party? Bullshit!" He slammed the door on his way out.

Chapter 43

Bristol was not considered to finish high in the table. Like most of the lower teams in the BFL, they relied on the running game with a stingy defense.

Bristol was quite the trek from Leeds, with players on the coach listening to music, watching movies on their laptops, avoiding the view of the cars flying by on the motorway. While it was a Sunday, traffic was still busy. With 35 million vehicles on UK roads each day, Sundays were only a light relief.

Harry had been thinking the entire trip about Amy. Her parents were awesome, making him feel so welcome, and the food … but he didn't like the way the visit had ended.

He completely hated the feeling of being jealous. He couldn't remember the last time he'd had such feelings. *Harry, mate, the thing about jealousy is not being self-confident enough. I usually am and all I need to do is be top dog again and kick some ass today. Show the coaches who should be the starting QB. Ben Shannon owns the Cougars but I will lead them all the fucking way to the top.* He felt better and would make sure he apologized to Amy.

Once they had exited the motorway, the view became serene, more peaceful. Players seemed to perk up, taking in the sunshine, greener views, and a welcome change from the horrendous traffic. For most of the players, this would be their first visit to the city, or even into the Southwest of England. Harry knew Bristol had won an award for the best green city. It was a large city, with knowledgeable football fans.

They arrived at the stadium with all the players in good spirits and headed for the dressing rooms. Harry finished up his stretch exercises, which all players did prior to a game, as quickly as possible. He liked to throw balls far more than exercise on game day. He noticed the small crowd. He gazed around, recalling some of his college games when 50,000 would be considered small. There couldn't be 10,000 here today and that with a bunch of Cougars fans making the journey. The crowd was not a patch on the Cougar Dome attendance, which in some ways would bring everybody back to reality.

I hate to admit it; Ben Shannon is a fucking genius. Our opening game was up there with the Raven's attendance, the champions, and that our first game. If only he would leave Amy alone, he would be a good bloke. What were his intentions?

Harry was charged up leaving the field and heading back into the dressing room, where Coach Greaves would give the usual pep talk. *This was easily the best he had felt about football in a year,* he decided.

He had a soft spot for the city of Bristol, something he would keep to himself for now. On the field however, given the opportunity, he would beat Bristol handsomely, showing the Cougars and the world: Harry Smith is back.

All the players seemed in fine form, joking around, talking about the game.

"After that hard game last week, this should be a walk in the park."

"Yeah. That fucking Ravens' defense is tough," said the running back.

He took in the atmosphere, the smell of sweat, the anticipation, and the players going through their various routines – some superstitious, on edge, while others relaxed, listening to music.

Coach Greaves came through the door, posted the starting 11 for both offense and defense on the wall.

"I'll be back in fifteen minutes for a final talk."

The guys all jumped up, checking out the team news. Brad was deadly quiet, studying the sheet, shaking his head. He went back to his locker, pulled out his helmet, tossing it full pelt across the room. A few players jumped out of the way as it crashed against the wall not too far from Harry.

"Hey, Brad! What the fuck is up with you?" Harry looked at him in surprise, feeling the whole room watching.

"You, as it happens. Thanks to your Cougar girl, I'm on the bench. This isn't right! I'm the starting QB of this team and I did put all the hard work against the Ravens. You came on for what? The final quarter?"

"Yeah, and won the game."

"I had the game all set up for you to win. Besides, the only reason you're starting today is down to the fact that you're fucking the Cougar girl."

"Say that again, asshole!" Harry yelled, rising from the bench.

"Yep. Maybe I'll have her next, then Leroy and the whole team by season's end. What do you Brits say? She's had more pricks than a pub dartboard."

Some of the players laughed, others watched Harry in

alarm as he flew across the room, landing a diving head-butt on the side of Brad's ear. They both went down, exchanging blows, the players jumping to their feet, coaches running through the door.

"What the hell is going on?"

Harry stood first. "It's just the normal pre-game tension, Coach. Nothing to worry about. Right, Brad?"

The other quarterback nodded.

As expected, Harry came out for the first play of the game. He stepped back, surveying the field. *Dammit, I'm taking far too long to make this play decision.* He looked for a slant pass to the slot receiver, generally an instinctive play that came naturally to Harry. One, two, three steps back.

Today, right now, he had other things on his mind. One split second he saw the receiver move, the next second his memory of Amy's face, looking so sad when he left the other night, slamming the door. Now Brad. *Next time he dogs Amy, I will put him in hospital.*

In this game at the position of QB, you rarely have three seconds, most times less than two. A Bristol linebacker saw a gap and took advantage of the opportunity to shoot straight up the middle, through the Cougar line. He barged into Harry with such force, his helmet directly impacting on Harry's shoulder.

"Shit!" Harry leapt up almost immediately, his arm shaking uncontrollably. He held it tight with his other arm. Brad came on the field.

"Shit out of luck, sucker."

"Fuck off."

Chapter 44

Amy and Paul could only look on in shock from the stands.

"That is all we needed," said Paul miserably.

Amy nodded with a sigh.

"He was just getting back to his old self. I watched him in training this week and the comeback final quarter in the opening game was just like Texas. I heard a rumor he was starting today thanks to the Cougar girl."

"Yes, but that's a sore point with the Cougar organization."

"Don't tell me: it's not what the fans want, it's the bloody coaches and their game plan."

"Yeah, something like that."

By half-time the Cougars were well on top, Brad playing a terrific first half. Amy and Paul headed for the dressing rooms to find Harry with his arm in a makeshift sling.

"I will take him to the hospital," Paul said. "Will you be okay on your own Amy? You don't need me for pointers. The Cougars will win this one handsomely."

"Of course. Text me once you know anything."

Paul could see Harry was totally dejected. He also wondered why there was little, if no, chemistry between him and Amy. They usually had eyes only for each other, but now they couldn't even meet each other's eyes.

Later, Paul was in the hospital waiting room – a place he'd rather not be, particularly with Harry. The thought of those days in hospital with Harry, in Texas, sent a shudder down his back.

His phone chimed with a text from Amy asking for an update. She also added that the game had finished with the Cougars winning 38-7.

Harry came out shortly with his arm in a sling.

"Please don't tell me it's broken."

"No, we are okay G Pops, just some heavy bruising. I will probably have to rest for a few weeks."

Paul sent Amy a text message. *Nothing broken, just some heavy bruising*, the message read.

Thank God for that, was her immediate reply.

Chapter 45

Amy arrived back late at her parents after the Bristol game. Tomorrow she should receive the all-clear from the hospital and be back in her own place next week. The mobile phone rang from its place on the charger. *Who is this so late?*

"Amy here," she answered curtly.

"It's Ben. Do you have a minute?"

"Sure. Kind of late. By the way, good win today."

"Thanks. I can't wait to read your report in the morning."

"It's already gone in, actually. The headline is 'Cougars miss Prince Harry'."

Ben's end of the line was dead silent.

"Just teasing," Amy finally admitted, although really she wanted to mess with him more.

"I wanted to ask if you would be my guest at a wine tasting tomorrow night. The host is a leading sommelier and friend of mine."

"May I invite Harry?"

Another pause.

"Well, there are only two seats left. It's sort of last minute. Besides, I thought Harry preferred beer. Not to mention he'll be sore for a few days."

"Okay, sure. I'll be there. Just text me the address. For now, I need to sleep."

Chapter 46

Amy arrived at the Imperial Hotel in Leeds. The hotel was by far the most elegant and expensive in West Yorkshire. Ben had sent his driver to pick her up, leaving a message that he would see her inside.

She found the room up a short flight of stairs from the main lobby. The tastefully decorated room had a long table with six glasses at each spot. She found her name tag at the top of the table next to Ben's.

God! This is going to be so pretentious, she thought. *All I want is some good wine.* She read the wine menu, which was written in gold typeface with extensive tasting notes for each wine. There was a blurb on the 2005 vintage, one of the best in modern time. On the page adjacent to the vintage notes was a terrific picture of the splendid Chateau Palmer estate.

Right – the makers of Altered Ego. Dad and I have had that one. We thought that was so expensive and yet it's cheap compared to the one on show this evening.

She continued to study the table setting. A small silver spit bucket was assigned for each person.

"Hell, you won't find me spitting this stuff out," she muttered decisively.

Ben arrived with a strange-looking guy in tow. He introduced his friend as Marcel, their wine expert and sommelier for the evening.

"I am delighted to meet you, mademoiselle."

She smiled back awkwardly. Marcel was French, wearing a medallion around his neck as big as his ego.

"All of the wines this evening are from the Bordeaux region, all the reds being from the 2005 vintage," he announced flamboyantly.

Ben leaned over, whispering to Amy, "I was missing one from my collection. Our fifth wine this evening. It comes from a small estate on The Left Bank. One is more Merlot than Cab and vice versa on The Right Bank, but I can never remember which way round."

"Impressive enough for me!"

"Most people – especially your age group – would not have a clue." He continued speaking under his breath, "I've already bought a few cases, and tonight's tasting will give me the opportunity to determine how much cellaring they require. By the way, we found my gift in the office and what a nice touch. My golfing buddies will be well impressed."

Amy nodded. She was totally out of her depth with this kind of wine knowledge. She opted for humour instead. "You are welcome for the gift. By the way, what is the stupid thing he has around his neck?"

Ben almost spilled his wine with a sudden laugh.

"Mr. Shannon, do you find the wine amusing?" Marcel looked down his award-winning nose at him.

"Yes, actually. It's a stunner. Its aroma of faint nectarines conjured up a special moment in my life – quite an amusing one. Pardon me for the distraction. Please continue, Marcel."

"Aren't we the bullshitter?" Amy whispered.

"Quick on my feet, more like."

Marcel encouraged the group to sample the last wine in the adjoining lounge area. Ben gave her his arm and leaned in to whisper in her ear.

"Amy, might we have a word in private?"

It was not a strange request – they had plenty of reason to talk business – but there was something odd about the way he asked.

They took a small table in the corner, Ben making eye contact with no one but Amy. "I have something important to ask. This would be such a big help and put our difficult conversation we had last week behind us."

"I am intrigued. Please, fire away."

"Harry's shoulder is not so good. The doctors said at least three weeks rest. I need you to write to the contrary."

Amy frowned, puzzled. "Harry's fine. He's itching to take the starting job back off Brad."

Ben pressed his lips together and gave a faint shake of his head.

"Enlighten me."

Ben sighed. "We don't want to be looking for a replacement this time of the year. By the time we have someone up to speed with our playbook, Harry will be fine. We have a third string utility player if necessary. I just prefer our opponents don't find out at this point. Who knows? He may be okay in a couple of weeks. I've taken care of the doctor – he happens to like fine wine. He will stay quiet on the subject."

"I don't like it, Ben. Who should I quote as my source that he's okay, ready to play?"

"Quote Harry, if you like. You already know what he'd say."

"Okay, let me think about it. In the meantime, would you get me a refill, darling?"

"Don't milk it." He chuckled and slipped off his chair. "I owe you, but I'm not your slave for life." He left for the bar area.

Just the opportunity I've been looking for, she thought.

Ben returned with more wine.

"Ben, before I give you an answer, I have a question. Why do you want me – someone you accused of being biased – to write a story?

"Let me put it this way. A year ago you were reporting on soccer games in the most undesirable of locations such as Barnsley. Today, I had a message from a colleague in Texas that had read one of your articles courtesy of the associated press. Damn! The US of A is hearing about the Cougars. They seem to like a young lady's perspective on the game. Sure. You've done remarkably well. Keep up the good work and I totally trust you moving forward."

"Thanks," said Amy. She smiled, her confidence returning now that the wine snobs were off chatting amongst themselves.

"So, why the question?"

"I want you to trust me fully moving forward with my reporting. You have my word I will not show any favoritism to Harry."

"Amy, I can't believe how good you are at this, your love of the game. You will single-handedly put the Cougars and UK American football on the world map." He leaned back and smiled. "By the way, how are you and Harry? He will be difficult to be around with the banged up shoulder."

"I took your advice and we've entered a cool period with a view to going wild somewhere exotic after the season is over. We are both focused on the Cougar season for now."

"You know, Amy, I have a vision, a project I am working on – please don't ask about it. When I succeed, you'll have the story first with a pile of jealous newspaper writers trailing after you. It will make your sacrifice to focus on your career all worthwhile. Harry will understand. You wait and see.

"This story – whatever it is – will be read both nationally and globally. I guarantee it."

Chapter 47

Harry was not in a good mood. His shoulder was killing him and he needed to get out, have a few pints.

Bloody bad timing when I was just getting to feel right and enjoy football again. Still, I didn't zone in, focus on the play, too much going through my mind. I will have to work on that.

Brad would have all the glory for beating Bristol. Thirty-eight points. *Fuck! I would have scored over fifty on that lot.*

He was browsing on the Internet, leaving Amy's daily article until last. Her story on the beginning of American football on UK soil was interesting, reminding him of all the stories G Pops had raised him on.

He'd called Amy, invited her for lunch – his treat – and apologized for storming out of her parents' house. He realized her career was just as important as his right now and he should be more supportive. Hell, he would be so happy right now to be with Amy every second of each and every day. *I have to get out of fantasy land, play great ball and watch Amy take the world by storm.*

She arrived on time wearing her usual work outfit: trousers, hair tied in a ponytail, taking off her flat cap as she entered the pub restaurant.

"How is the shoulder?" she asked.

"Sore and making me grumpy. I thought seeing you would cheer me up."

"And?"

"Of course seeing you would always cheer me up, but I have to apologize first. Sorry Amy and I mean it."

"What are you saying sorry for precisely?"

Oh fuck, I hate it when girls can't just accept sorry, requiring a full account of why we're dick heads. Harry cleared his throat, "I fully support you in your career and I don't get to control who you see."

"Not bad for a guy," she said with a faint smile. "I am not seeing anyone else but you. Yes, I will see friends of both sexes when I please. Just get through your thick skull that my friendship with Ben is totally platonic. So, when do you think you will be back throwing a ball?"

"That's the thing about football, Amy. It's a game of inches and seconds, with a short career span. The hit on my shoulder could have been much worse. You always need a plan B."

"Do you have one? Like finishing your degree?"

"Something like that," he agreed, with a smile. "What about you. Have you ever thought about the future? Kids? Settling down?"

"Yeah. No doubt in my mind once I get into my thirties. I would like one of each, a boy and a girl. I want to take my career to the top, see how far I can go before having a few years off for a family. It would be good to find the right guy to have a family with, and to be honest, I don't have a lot of trust in guys from my limited experience."

Harry looked away.

"Oh! I don't mean you. Shit, we just had our first tiff. I am a right pain with the whole Cougar girl thing right now.

I just hope you'll support me. I can switch off occasionally to have time with you, I promise." However, she let the word hang for a moment. "You do seem to bring up sex every time we talk. I was hoping we had more to this relationship than that. Still, whatever."

Harry gazed into her eyes, her beautiful face. Her jaw had turned yellow from the heavy bruising she had sustained by the nasty bastard that was in Ben's office. He held her hand tightly, not allowing her to move. "Ever since we met, our lives have been a whirlwind. Shit! We talk about the Cougars and my stupid shoulder. Amy, how are you feeling after the accident? Do you still have many bruises?"

She touched her face with her other hand. "My jaw is still sore and I have headaches. Hey, thanks for asking. You're right: life is a roller coaster ride these days."

"Well, being with you is not all about sex. I feel good with you. You help me switch off from the craziness."

"You do, too," she agreed.

Their plates empty and all the words said, Amy took her hand back. "I've got to go. Thanks for lunch. My place this weekend? I'll cook you a meal to surpass my mum's and supply the wine." She kissed him hard on the lips.

He watched her Mini Cooper set off with a wheel spin, the sound of the gears changing at a speed that reminded him of Formula One. He never did feel safe driving with Amy.

Well, that went according to plan. He would be her husband, father her two kids – he knew it, one day down the road. She was the one for him. All he needed to do now is stop playing the silly bugger and sort out this thing she had for Ben Shannon.

Chapter 48

Ben checked his monitor to find Raymond displayed there, drinking a mug of coffee.

"How long have you been waiting for me?"

"Oh, just a few minutes. I'm reflecting on this wonderful morning in sunny Stamford. Had my run in the park down by the river."

"Okay, enough. Why are you really so happy this morning? You have good news?"

"They are a match."

"Bloody hell! Give me a short version of how you pulled it off. I know what you're like. Your reports read like *Gone with the Wind*."

"Finding a way to get a sample from Penny took me almost a week. I followed her every morning to the coffee shop near her school. Security was relaxed enough in the village for me to pick my moment to switch coffee mugs without any suspicion.

"Bazan was fortunately sloppy in his early days. I called in a favor to one of my old government colleagues, who managed to get us in the cold case files building. You can get a DNA sample tested for almost the slightest trace these days. Not like the nineties when Bazan began his evil empire of crime."

"100% conclusive for sure?"

"Yes. Denis Bazan is Penny Davenport's biological father. This would be devastating for the family and the government, with Sir Geoffrey and her being so tight."

Ben nodded.

"They are both accomplished sailors – they won that yacht race last year. He watches many of her tennis games."

"A junior champ, right?"

"Yes, Ben. This is huge. What will you do with it?"

"All I want is for Bazan to play fair in the game of football. If he came at me on the business side, or if he had intended to hurt Amy, I would tear him apart – probably have him taken out permanently."

"You know that can always be arranged. Just give me the word, anytime."

With this information in his back pocket, all he hoped for this year was to win the bowl, beat the Ravens and ram it down Bazan's throat. Make the folks back in the USA sit up and take notice. He clicked on the Gazette website he had bookmarked to read Amy's latest installment.

Chapter 49

Harry couldn't stand it any longer!

He hardly slept all night, thinking about Amy with Ben.

She had called him raving about some wine function. "The 2005 vintage was out of this world."

"Why didn't I get an invitation?" he had asked.

"Last minute, only one seat, you are not a wine person." *Blah blah fucking blah.*

The next day, trying his best to throw pass after pass in training, knowing Ben was right there in his fucking office looking down on him, was more than he could take. He decided tonight he would confront him. *Multi-millionaires don't worry me, I almost fucking died!*

He grabbed a taxi outside. After telling Ben exactly what was in his mind, he would head back to the city and get absolutely smashed out of his mind drunk and maybe head to a nightclub and find a girl to take home. *Fuck the lot of 'em!*

Harry arrived at the gate to Ben's house and pushed the button. Nothing. On the third attempt, the intercom came to life.

"Mr. Shannon? It's Harry Smith. I would like to speak with you please."

No reply.

"If you want me to keep up with this shoulder injury bullshit, you will speak with me! No more BS, Ben. Open the gate."

The gate opened. Harry walked through the front door, which was open wide. He walked through two rooms and followed the sound of some new Texan Country superstar singing a song about tornadoes. He paused, lost composure, fell into a flashback of his accident.

It was only ice. You should have had your A-game driving that morning, instead of thinking about fucking tornadoes.

"What the hell are you doing coming here – to my house – on this day?"

Harry sparked back to reality. "What day?" He looked around the room. There was Ben in just a pair of jeans, no socks or shirt. The smell of booze filled his nose like he was on a distillery tour.

"Where's the staff? I heard you had a house full of them." At the sight of his boss in such a state, all the fury went out of Harry.

"Gave them all the day off. I don't want anybody here today and that includes you. If you have to be here, pour yourself a drink and get me a refill." Harry poured a scotch from the kitchen, walked back into the room and found the mute button on the remote.

"Mr. Shannon?"

"Call me Ben."

"Ben, I need to talk with you. This is very important to me, but if this is a bad time?"

Ben seemed to sober up somewhat.

"Is this about your playing? Harry, you're doing okay.

Not the guy I saw in Texas but I trust you. If anything happens to Brad, you will be our guy. Our Comeback Kid."

"I'm not here to talk about football."

Ben turned suddenly and almost fell off the sofa.

"Not football? Why else would you come out here?"

"It's about Amy."

Ben leapt from the sofa and went into the kitchen. "I need coffee fast. What the hell has happened to Amy after all she has just been through?"

"Ben, sit down. I'll make the coffee. Nothing is wrong with Amy. Please relax."

Ben looked puzzled and sat on a bar stool with his elbows on the counter.

"This is so hard for me to say, but here it is. I think the two of you are having an affair – you and Amy. Mr. Shannon – Ben – it's just not right! We have a future – I'm sure of it."

"Oh God, lad! You know what thought did: followed a muck cart and thought it was a wedding!"

"Seems you've been away from Texas too long. I've heard you lot up here use that odd saying," he mumbled, feeling embarrassed.

"You sound like my old mum. Now forget the coffee, get me another scotch. You're right – we do need to talk!"

Back on the sofa, Ben squeezed Harry's shoulder.

"Buddy, you have it all wrong. I swear. Amy is just a good friend. I like her, respect her, but not in the way you're thinking."

"Well, what about Amy and her feelings for you?"

"I don't think so. She hinted to me about her fondness for you quite some time ago."

"Really?" he said with a faint smile. "Ben, could you be sending her mixed messages?"

Ben poured another scotch. Tears developed in his eyes. "Want to know why I am drunk tonight, son? It's our 20th anniversary." He picked up a photograph from the mantel piece.

"I never knew you were married. Where is she?"

"Somewhere in Arizona. I've hardly seen her in almost twenty years."

Harry looked puzzled.

"It's not our wedding anniversary. twenty years ago to the day since we lost our daughter." He held out the photo – showing a sleeping baby in a pink blanket.

"Oh shit!"

"After she died, I decided to work hard, focus on my career, build an empire. It was the only thing to keep me level-headed. My wife and I hardly saw each other. In the end she went to some commune out in the desert. I tried going to see her a few times," he paused, choking back the tears. "I always wanted a daughter. Our family going way back was all boys, and I missed not having a sister growing up. We got the news she was a girl when my wife was seven months pregnant. I went to town buying everything pink. There were complications at birth. I got to hold her, see her face.

"Each year I get into this state, usually take the day off. On this day each year I visualize what Renee would be like. She would have been twenty today, four years younger than Amy. She would have had her mother's looks; Spanish, so gorgeous, and she would have had my personality, confidence, stubborn as hell." He forced a smile.

The lights came on. Harry realized. "Amy?"

"Dead straight."

He pressed the remote, scrolling down the menu. "Watch some football with me."

"Man! Now I feel like shit, getting all of this back to front."

"No sweat. You love her, man. Now let's see if I can find a Patriot game for you. Otherwise, I have lots of Houston." Ben flicked around on the remote. "Hey, question: do you play golf? Only I've never seen you with the other players and I wondered, since you lived in Texas with all the fine courses and great weather."

"Yeah, I wasn't half bad a few years ago. I haven't picked up my clubs in over a year. I think they are at my parents'. Why do you ask?"

"I'm a member at Chapel Allerton club. Tomorrow afternoon there's a big tournament. Been a member since I was very young and this is too important to let them down. Trouble is, my team needs a fourth player." Ben looked at him expectantly.

After the accusations he'd made, how could Harry refuse?

Chapter 50

Harry fell on the bed exhausted back at his flat, his mind racing with the events of this evening at Ben's. How could he have been such a twit? Ben is a great guy and hurting inside. He found the remote to his iPod docking station and kept hitting the button. He was not in the mood for new stuff and switched to a local radio station. A soft sexy voice was singing a cover to an old song from U2's *Joshua Tree* album. He smiled wondering how his dad and G Pops would critique the new cover. They frigging loved U2.

He heard the girl sing, "We run like a river runs to the sea." The lyrics conjured up images of Amy, Ben, G Pops and him all going to the same place: the bowl championship. Amy immediately popped into his mind, looking as gorgeous as ever. He would finish the season with the MVP and whisk Amy off somewhere exotic, just the two of them.

He looked at his watch – midnight – shook his head, and then changed his mind. Amy came up on his phone screen. He answered it with a smile.

"Hey, just on my way to bed, what's up calling me at midnight and on video conferencing?"

"I wanted to see you, not just hear your voice. You mind? Actually, I was just thinking about you and how my idea of cooling things off until the end of the season was proper daft!"

"Glad, you worked that out. I'll be round in twenty minutes."

"Not so fast tiger. How about dinner tomorrow night? I'm cooking and you can bring your toothbrush for the morning."

"24 hours? I will never survive practice tomorrow thinking about being with you."

"Tough and by the way it's not twenty-four hours, since you called me at midnight. I have a big day tomorrow with my new football education blog."

I have golf in the morning, probably not a good idea to spend the early morning with Amy. We would make love for hours with little sleep, and in the morning she would attack me in the shower, putting an end to my golf game.

"You seem really chirpy. What's being going on? Been in the pub?"

"No. Had a few drinks here watching telly, doing some thinking."

"Not too heavy I hope."

"Well, first I decided Brad is a prick. So I plan on taking his job starting for the Cougars… Also, being jealous about Ben was dumb. I like everything about you and not just your amazing body." He couldn't tell her he'd also been thinking about his visit with Ben and his secret. He would have to at some point, but not now.

"Wow, what a night of reflection! Were you doing any pot?"

"Very funny."

"I won't keep you. Just wanted to invite you to dinner. Now go to bed with this thought." Harry watched while she propped up her phone on the table, turned her back to the phone, walked slowly in a sexy style into the middle of the room. She took off her t-shirt, turned to the phone, walking back towards the table. Harry stared while her breasts finally touched the screen.

"Amy, you are such a fucking tease."

"Nighty night, Harry," she said giggling. The call ended.

Man, he would never sleep tonight with thoughts of Amy dancing like that. Thoughts of tomorrow night and Amy dancing around the room for him appeared in his mind. He decided on a cold shower.

Chapter 51

Amy was in the office checking her blog comments. *So much Twitter activity!* She'd arrived early for a change. Excited, apprehensive – hell – she'd tossed and turned all night. Between her popularity soaring on her blog, and calling Harry at midnight, she was too preoccupied to sleep. But while the sleep was not forthcoming, she did feel on cloud nine.

Her story on the history of American football in the UK was gaining traction.

She had started a thread on Twitter after covering the 1986 opening season. One thing she'd learned in her profession was that when it comes to social networking, make your audience a part of the team. *'What is your favourite year in sports to date?'* she'd asked them. She'd had literally thousands of replies with many amazing stories.

Some were personal, from fans participating in the paraplegic games or climbing a mountain, to others that just reminisced about their favorite team. She had received many from Bradford City fans on their Wembley run in 2013, how they loved being the giant killers only to be beaten severely at Wembley by Premier side Swansea, immediately followed by another rare opportunity to go back and win promotion at the same prestigious venue. A lowly team at Wembley twice in one year was unheard of.

Her educational blog on the ins and outs of the game had been breathtaking with all the responses and followers. It was now being viewed globally by the under-thirty crowd, who appreciated Amy's comments and the way she had started with zero knowledge of the game.

She'd got the inspiration from watching those Super Bowl games with her dad. He was enjoying the game to a point, but kept asking the TV screen, "Why did you do that?" Amy decided the fans needed to know the basics. She had sent out a questionnaire on her blog which was linked to all the social networking media. The number one question she received back was, *'What do the players talk about in the huddle? Do they have a chat between each play?'* Fans jumped on the question with many variations of suggestions, some funny – *'let's have a pot of tea'* – others vulgar or completely zany.

So she set out to educate with a fun, direct approach. The game of American football was the only game in the world that was influenced to such an extent by the coaches. In fact, they drew up all the plays ahead of time, each play having a name. All the players in training camp would have to study all the plays.

Then the coaches would decide what plays to employ. In the earlier days before a microphone in the QB's helmet, this would be a hand signal from the coach. For the play 22 dive on 2, he would show two fingers twice followed by a fist. Opposing teams designed spying techniques to see the hand signals and hence communication through the helmet became necessary.

The QB would huddle up the players, shouting 22 dive on 2, for example. This would mean the second running back would run with the ball through the second hole. There are usually two linemen on either side of the centre, the guy that has the ball, with the QB bent behind him to receive the ball. In between each lineman is a gap which is numbered. Two is the first gap on the right-hand side between the centre and the first lineman. On 2 is when the QB shouts "hut, hut". The linemen need to know this so they don't move too quick and become offside. Simple, yeah?

Not bloody likely, she thought.

The only time this could change is when the QB spots a change on the defense formation and deems the coach's play would not be successful. He then calls an audible. Let's say the colour chosen for the day is red, and the state Nebraska. So he calls red, Nebraska, 22 dive on 2, usually repeating himself to make sure the players have it their minds. On an audible, it may be green, Ohio, 25 on two. They might change to the third gap on the left-hand side for the running back.

Once Amy had studied the game, it was relatively easy to understand the basics. Conveying them on her blog was far more difficult than she had imagined. She decided to build a YouTube channel and, while she was still nervous at the thought of being on camera, showing the basic plays really worked. She had graphs showing the line with numbers for the gaps. Behind her she had set up Apple TV with a large screen where she had picked various plays from the BFL and NFL games. Her followers totally bought into the YouTube idea with tweets galore: *Check out the Cougar girl channel!* She would have to think about having guests on her new show soon.

Her workmates filtered into the office one by one. Gone were the sarcastic comments, although they still referred to her as AC. She quite liked it.

"AC, nice story!" said more than one voice.

Her boss opened the door with a wave to summon her into his wonderful office, no doubt for another talk about high expense accounts. She smiled, pointing her finger to her chest in question. He waved his hand with a gesture that seemed to say, "Stop fooling around."

"Good morning, boss." She closed the door and sat down opposite him.

"Did you bring me a coffee this morning?"

She smiled with no reply.

"The Gazette board of directors can't get enough of you, Amy. Do I get some credit here for making you our Cougar girl?"

"Boss, all the compliments in the world won't put food on the table. How about a pay increase? And while we're at it, you could be more lenient with my expense account."

"Trouble is the BFL is such a short season. What are we going to do with you? They are nominating you for young journalist of the year, for goodness sake! We've only ever had two nominees and no winners. Never in our wildest dreams would we have expected a sports writer to have a chance."

She had not considered the short season, or what to do after it had finished. After all, she worked all year with the Gazette. She'd been so busy enjoying this whirlwind rise to notoriety in such a short space of time, that she hadn't seen the end of the whirlwind coming.

"Can we think about that when the time comes, boss? I'm so focused right now."

"Of course, Amy. Keep up the good work, Cougar girl."

Chapter 52

Ben arrived at the old Masonic building in the Bayswater district of West London. He told his driver to have a meal, look out for his text message and that he'd probably be two or three hours. He pressed the buzzer. The door unlocked, revealing an old foyer with cage lifts he hadn't seen in years. *Are those things safe?* He opted for the stairs, climbing two steps at a time.

In the main area he found most of the BFL owners, along with other officials who would be part of the agenda for the meeting. Since the higher-ups had determined the officials were slowing down the game, this was the number one issue on the agenda. They would then send out the officials and close the doors to everybody but the owners. The big eight would be left to do battle with the other issues.

Ben strolled around the room, stopping to gaze at the Masonic windows. The knowing Eye was at the top of the square, the eye that appears on the American one-dollar bill. In the centre of the square was the Masonic symbol with the square and compass. The Eye was creepy, following his every move. He imagined how many Americans have a one-dollar bill in their wallet, in the house – in fact, everywhere.

He knew enough about the all-seeing Eye of god. To the USA it meant, "New Order of the Ages". The Eye was positioned above a pyramid with thirteen steps, representing the original thirteen states and the future growth of the country. Franklin and Hancock, to name a couple of the many founding fathers of the USA, subscribed to this view. Masons, on the other hand, adopted the Eye of god to be a symbol for his care and watchfulness over the entire universe.

He had been initiated and given a card – *Apprentice Mason* – at a lodge in Houston. He'd initially thought it would be good for social networking. After all, some of the most famous men in history were Masons, on both sides of the pond. Churchill, Newton, the Kings of England, so many US presidents, J. Edgar Hoover – the list was endless.

He had always wondered what happened at the 32nd degree. His dad had made it to a prominent Worshipful Master and Knight Templar in his day. Something about that level stayed a secret, and his dad was revealing nothing. He never liked the blindfold, the hood – he'd been scared of the dark since he was a kid. Fear of going blind – it wasn't a good feeling. The rest was just like a good frat initiation at college – the rolled-up trouser leg, noose hanging loose around your neck. Only the blindness unnerved him, men watching, talking, while he was in total darkness.

Bazan entered the room and shook hands with the BFL president. He was too far away to study the handshake, but would bet Bazan was a Mason. The thumb and third finger would be pressing in just the right spots. *Damn, I can even remember it these days. Something about there being twelve signs of recognition between the Mason brothers.* He pondered, finally giving up trying to rack his brains.

Time for some fun, he decided. He walked into the room,

nodding with a smile at the group seated around the long table, an expensive leather briefcase in his left hand.

They discussed the constant throwing of the duster by officials, particularly on kick returns.

"Clipping is illegal," the officials protested. "What do you want to us to do? It's the rules."

The discussion seemed to be going nowhere, but after the team owners argued that flow of the game was vital to its success and total acceptance in the UK, the officials promised to be a tad more lenient in the future.

The owners all decided to take a fifteen-minute break before addressing the main topic of the NFL on UK soil.

Ben took in the scene. The whole group went to the bar for refills, except Bazan, who was heading to the toilet. He had only one bodyguard with him, loitering around the hall, popping his head around the main door before they had gone into the meeting.

He slipped in the toilet to see only Bazan, leaning over the urinal.

"Come on you bastard! Work!"

"Denis, you really need to see a doc about that prostate problem."

Denis kept perfectly still, still facing the wall. "What the fuck do you want?"

"I have a surprise for you: some information you'll love to see." Ben stayed put while Denis turned, zipped up his trousers and slowly moved to the basins.

After he'd washed his hands, Ben passed him a file. Denis opened the folder, the frown on his forehead becoming deeper, his face red, veins on his neck now bulging. He loosened his tie. When Denis finally made eye contact, Ben hit him hard in the stomach.

"That's for Amy Carrington."

Denis groaned loud, too loud. The goon barged through the door.

"What the fuck? I will have you mate."

Ben made a firm stance with his feet, ready to take him on.

"Stop right there, you wanker!" Denis groaned. "Leave us now." The bodyguard looked skeptical, but obeyed. "Look, Shannon, the girl was an accident, just doing some snooping – yer know, Cougar playbook, all that stuff. Shit! I've even started reading her fucking stories. I never meant her any harm, mate."

"Well, whatever your intentions, harm is what you caused. I can't have you fucking with my friends, the Cougar organization or anything that I hold important in life. We have professional whistleblowers in place ready to leak this story to the papers by morning."

"What do you want, mate? An apology?"

"No, actually. Believe it or not, I need you focused on the future of the Ravens. All clean and above board, with no funny stuff. The NFL is looking at us, Bazan – you, me and Manchester – the three teams that have potential to be a part of the NFL. Let me down and I will personally destroy you. Clear?"

Denis nodded, not making eye contact.

"Tomorrow's game will have a huge impact on the season. I hear there will be representatives from the NFL in the crowd. If the game is anything like our first game at the dome, they will be suitably impressed."

"You have my word," Bazan growled. "All above board from now on."

Ben turned to the door.

"Hey Shannon! We will beat your Cougars tomorrow. No team ever beats us in our own manor."

And the Ravens did, decisively.

Chapter 53

Harry sat on the coach. He turned around to see the lights of London in the rear window, becoming smaller, further away in the distance.

Fucking London! Those bloody Ravens!

He was convinced they could do it. Come from behind: Harry the Comeback Kid, Brad the stylish pocket QB. They were the dynamic duo, the two of them. He still hated Brad's guts. He would not forgive him for what he'd said about Amy. Any more bad-mouthing and he would smack the shit out of him. However, in the BFL there was no other double threat quite like the two of them and he liked it.

What went wrong? He could see Amy's report in the morning paper. He dreaded the thought of reading it. But he would, of course, never miss a word she wrote. *Where was the Comeback Kid?*

Well, fuck! I should have done it. I like all that pressure. I focus, my mind is clearer, faster. But that bloody defense. That would be a good story: the fucking iron curtain, no way through.

He thought about the comeback scenario, why he seemed to play so much better. Thinking back to his first years at school, those report cards that would always carry the same message: *Harry has so much potential. However, he can't focus on one subject. His mind wanders too much from the task at hand.* He had always been that way.

So how the hell did he conquer it in Texas? He thought hard. *I don't know, can't remember even playing in Texas.* He thought about the day everything changed for him, still trying to recall the actual accident. Nothing!

Fuck! How do we beat the Ravens in the bowl final? There you go again, Harry: thinking too far ahead. We have to beat Manchester first!

Part 4

Chapter 54

Ben was reading Amy's story on yesterday's game, pausing to study the league table she had included in the match report. Ravens were on top, with only one loss coming on the opening day right there at the Cougar Dome. Gladiators and Cougars were tied for second. Gladiators had lost both games against the Ravens, while his team had lost in both London and Manchester.

Back-to-back losses. *Shit*! At the time he'd been seething, having to keep his utter disappointment and anger under control. First thing after the Ravens loss, he'd called a closed-door meeting with the coaches.

"Gentlemen, we were put in our places on Sunday. The rookies of the league were given a lesson by the seasoned champs. After this conversation, I don't want to hear the word Ravens mentioned again in the regular season. We tried both quarterbacks, changed defense strategy numerous times and all to no avail. Today we have one goal – do not lose another game for the rest of this season. We have Manchester twice, home and away. We must beat them and finish the season tied for first place. At that time, we have two weeks off to prepare for the bowl game. We will prepare like never before; we will work all of those fourteen days, 24/7 if necessary. Do I make myself clear?"

"Yes, Mr. Shannon," the coaches said confidently.

A week later, the next day after a loss at Manchester, he called a special meeting with coaches and players. Brad spoke up at the meeting.

"We have a quarterback controversy, Mr. Shannon."

Harry argued, "We have the best two QBs in the league – a double weapon. Brad, you're talking a load of bollocks."

"You remind me of Doug Flutie with the Buffalo Bills, coming in all the time, disrupting the team chemistry. Yep, just like him, you fucking midget!" yelled Brad.

"I hardly think 6 feet is short, you lanky piece of shit. Let's go right here!" Harry shouted back, his fists clenched tightly.

Nobody saw the moment of decision, but suddenly their two star quarterbacks were on each other, raining blows.

The coaches pulled them apart, while Ben looked on in total disbelief.

What have we done?

As soon as order reigned again, Ben spoke quietly, "There will be no QB controversy on this team, gentlemen. The coaches have Brad as starting QB with Harry on the sideline. You two, get over it and behave like men." He turned his attention to the entire room.

"The truth is, currently this team could not beat the Ravens without a miracle. Sure, we beat them in the opener, but they have adapted to Harry's comeback style. They seemed to have Brad's number from the start of the season. We need more plays, new plays they don't know or will never find out about. I have tighter security in the dome and we've revamped our entire computer system. Brad, it might be hard for you to admit, but Harry could be the key here."

Ben's speech was interrupted by a message from Andy. Andy's project had sent him to the USA, specifically the capital, to close a big deal involving Ben's companies, which had just launched a cutting-edge stock fund, and to keep an eye on the latest NFL news in his spare time.

Ben dismissed the meeting and sat down at his desk to call Andy. His face appeared on the screen within seconds.

"Andy, I can tell you have some news. I haven't seen you look this excited in a while. Spit it out lad."

"Ben, I believe your senator friend has been successful with the Sherman act."

"Bloody hell! You have to be kidding. After what, forty-four years? This could be the opening we have been looking for, Andy."

"Yeah boss, the NFL in the UK!"

"Keep me up to speed. Good work. I can handle it from here; keep working on the fund project."

Damn, this is big for the NFL.

Since 1974, fans wishing to buy season tickets had also been required to buy tickets for two preseason exhibition games at the same price. Fans hardly gave a damn about these games and yet they were forced to buy tickets regardless. Fact is, the players and coaches couldn't stand them either. Their salaries didn't kick in until the regular season started and consequently they were paid peanuts for those games. There were four in all, two at home and two away. This arrangement didn't suit anyone except for the team owners.

The controversy had gone all the way to the Supreme Court and, since a compromise was never found, the result was always in favor of the NFL teams. In 2008, the commissioner had tried an idea to shorten the preseason and extend the regular season by two games. The player's association squashed that idea and fast. If anything, they had proposed a shorter season due to current injury concerns and fatigue. This was the most physical game on the planet, they argued, and while fans would love to see more regular season games, they realized this was a full-contact sport.

Ben's solution was simple: come to England for the preseason games. Take it as a holiday leading up to the season. Fans in the UK would still see their favorite teams, get a look at the new drafted rookies and free agency signings, and at least a peek at their idols even if they only played one quarter per game. The Cougar Dome could host four games, dead easy. It would be the ultimate draw for new American Football fans – NFL teams in the UK!

They could have four preseason and two regular games at the dome. In a nutshell – UK farm teams, aligned to an NFL team, six possible games per season, counting the four preseason games, at the Cougar Dome. This was the answer for Britain, rather than the odd Wembley game with different teams each year. What the UK fans needed was their own identity where the NFL team could be thought of as a big brother.

In the meantime, this latest news gave Ben the impetus he needed to continue with his plan.

Chapter 55

Ben got Denis Bazan on his monitor. "Good day, old buddy. How are things in London?"

"What the fuck are you doing on my private Skype account?"

"Now come on, Denis. You know we don't have any secrets between us. By the way, good game the other week. Your defense seemed to know what we were doing for the entire game."

"What the fuck do you want Shannon? You'd better tell me before I have my techs come in here and change the account."

"My apologies for spoiling your Monday. Now shut up, you bastard, and listen up." His voice grew serious. "My sources tell me you are close to a deal with America's team for the first NFL franchise in the UK."

"Load of bollocks, has been for years. There will be no fucking cowboys in London mate. Bad enough we have to put up with seeing you down here. Thank fuck it's not more often, Tex."

"Denis, give up with the BS for once. You will do it this time. The deal will be sweeter and we both know you have problems with cash flow. Seems the Russians and Chinese are taking over your precious London. Still, if you still don't wish to be a part of Dallas, its fine, Denis. By all means, resist the temptation and carry on with your London Ravens. I'll do it right here. Leeds will not only be the cock of the North, we will represent the entire country. The first NFL team in the UK, right here in the best city in the country – Leeds."

"Fuck off." The monitor went to a blank screen.

I believe that will be a successful misdirection play.

Chapter 56

Amy wrote a pregame story. This was the big one to decide the Cougars' fate in their first season.

The season had gone close to form, with the exception of the big upset on opening day at the Cougar Dome. The Ravens, as usual, were never expected to lose a single game. Two national magazines had predicted Gladiators would be second, with the Cougars third. The Cougars were tied for second, with two losses each. The game in Manchester had been close. The coaches had been reluctant to send in Harry, since his shoulder was still sore from the Bristol game. Brad almost pulled it off in the final moments. But the Cougars' field goal kicker missed a 30-yard kick to lose the game in the dying seconds.

The rivalry between the two Northern cities went way back, a fierce sense of pride from a long and unfortunately violent history. Amy kept away from the soccer thug stories, making her piece far more lighthearted, with reference to Emmerdale Farm and Corrie and some of the best musicians. But, of course, she did mention Leeds had become the top city in the North.

She predicted the next game would be a low scoring affair with some special tips to watch on defense. She described in depth the secondary playing in a zone defense, working on split-second timing to execute fierce hits on the receivers.

Most of the season, the Cougars had scored at will by resounding margins. The Ravens and Gladiators were the exception with well-coached, disciplined D's. Brad would start with Harry ready. His shoulder was absolutely fine, and all the other Cougar players were fit and ready to go.

Chapter 57

Harry was totally revved up for this game.

One fucking mistake, Brad Douglas, and I will be in the game, cleaning up your mess once again. I'll show you. I'll take us to the bowl.

He felt alive, his brain sharper than ever. There would be no distractions today. He was in a great place with Amy; his game had improved no end. The crowd today had exceeded all expectations, with over 40,000 in attendance. He would have no mental distractions if he was given the opportunity to be in this game, none! Life was bloody brilliant with Amy after he had seen Ben, made the phone call and dinner the night after. The sex was unbelievable as usual, but there seemed to be a stronger connection between them.

Harry paced up and down the sideline as play began, the ball moving up and down the field. *We're not getting anywhere! The Gladiators have adopted the exact same defense as the Ravens. No way is Brad the dick scoring on them.*

This was too painful for Harry to watch. The game was a dreary stalemate.

At half-time, the game was tied at 7-7 apiece. Harry started bugging the coaches, "Let me get in there! I can win this game!"

Brad overheard him and yelled, "Shut the fuck up!"

"The whole season is riding on this game." Harry ignored Brad, pleading with the coaches, "I can do it. Get me in the game." His mind was sharper than ever since his accident. Plays flashed in his head. At last, the old Harry was beginning to emerge.

By the end of the third quarter, the score had not changed. Again he begged the coaches to no avail.

"Brad is our starter," they said. "We will score. Just be patient."

Deep into the fourth quarter, Manchester scored a field goal to take the lead to 10-7. With two minutes left, Brad had to conjure up the drive of his life. It was first and ten on their own 20-yard line, with time running out, their season on the line. The fans were quiet, no singing today. Their travel arrangements to Wembley, a weekend in the capital, hung in the balance of this one play.

Brad stepped back, looked right, and then left, poised to throw. Then he was hit hard, blindsided by the defensive end coming in at the speed of an express train. It was a low illegal hit, the helmet making direct contact with Brad's right knee. Brad did not get up.

The fans jumped to their feet, the players too. Harry stood as the stretcher came onto the field. Brad's groans could be heard around the dome in the horrified silence.

At a nod from the coaches, Harry came on and acted quickly. He couldn't spare any thoughts for Brad, how it must feel. He had to focus on this drive. He made two short passes for a fourth and 1 yard to go for a first down. The coaches sent in a full back.

Okay, I guess no decision for me. I could have tried a trick play, statue of liberty or something. Now the defense will be stacked to stop the running back.

A thought came into mind, and Harry turned it to action. They huddled up, 21 on 2. The play would be both backs running through the one hole, with the full back leading the way to make room. If he had told them his new plan, the players would have reacted differently, making the defense aware something could be afoot.

"Hut, hut!" he shouted, taking the ball, the full back running through the hole like a bulldozer, the running back coming up behind him, his hands ready for the ball.

Harry pushed the ball to him, into his hands, tight together in the middle of his chest. At the last second, he took the ball back and headed around the outside right, sprinting upfield.

Leroy, the college-star wide receiver, had spotted the change of play, putting a severe block on the cornerback. Harry continued upfield, speeding into the end zone.

TOUCHDOWN!

The fans went wild. Yet again, Harry was the Comeback Kid.

He would hear it from the coach; they never did like the QB making such an important decision on his own.

Coach Greaves was waiting for Harry on the sideline, pulling his arm while he tried to run past. He was expecting a total bollocking regardless of the fact he had won them the game.

"Harry, get ready for London in two weeks."

"What? Coach, I will be starting?"

"Brad is done this year. His knee is totally shot!"

Oh fuck, here is my chance.

Chapter 58

Ben was in his office raring to go. His mind was racing with the unique opportunity facing him. He called the Houston Texans.

"Connie, good morning. How is Houston on this fine morning?"

"Very hot, Mr. Shannon. I am afraid Bob is tied up in meetings all day. I have made him aware several times you've been calling. It seems to be overly busy around here this week."

"Will he be in Houston all week?"

"Yes, I believe he will."

"Thanks, Connie."

"Would you like to leave him a message?"

"Bob knows exactly why I'm calling. We're in the bowl and yet they're still stalling." Ben shook his head in disgust. "Well, I also know how to play this game."

He hung up and called his pilot, "Pack a bag and have my plane ready. We're going to Houston, today!"

Hours later, his pilot checked in with the Nova Scotia traffic controller with a clear path over the States down into Texas. The weather was sunny at 92 degrees Fahrenheit. He'd worked for the last six hours over the ocean and would now relax, excited to be heading back, even if only for a brief time.

The Texans were the team he desired. He'd been a big

fan of the Oilers in the nineties, but he could not follow his allegiance when they left for Tennessee. Instead, he'd waited five years for a new NFL team in Houston. Finally, a new stadium was built for the Texans downtown: the Astrodome, now a forgotten treasure in the sporting world.

The old dome had been a magnificent place – some said the eighth wonder of the world – when it was built in 1965. Ben reckoned he had seen just about everything in football at that stadium. Well, except the Oilers going to the Super Bowl. Buddy Ryan smacking his own fellow coach on the sideline; the bitter battles between coaches Glanville and Wyche of the Bengals; Warren Moon throwing 400 yards per game at will.

Still, his worst memory was watching his beloved team in the local sports bar with all his university mates, only to witness the Bills enjoy the biggest comeback in NFL history. It was an embarrassment the Oilers would never be allowed to forget.

He could remember so clearly buying a beer at half-time, laughing with all of his mates. 28-3 at half-time. The game was in the bag. Then the Bills scored 28 points in third quarter and went on to win 41-38. It was a lesson he learned, and something he used to this day in business and life in general: *Never assume*.

That was still in his mind as Ben arrived at the Houston Texans HQ, strolling into the lobby. He looked over to the large desk where Connie sat. He liked Connie, the gatekeeper. He had spoken to her many times on the phone and by email. She was difficult to read, kept everything completely professional. As he neared the desk, he was stunned to see she was extremely attractive, probably around 35, with no wedding ring.

"Good afternoon. Ben Shannon here to see Bob."

Connie looked flustered.

"Nice to finally meet you, Mr. Shannon. However, you don't have an appointment with Bob today."

"I know. Just flew in from England on an urgent matter. If you would let him know I will be sitting out here until he sees me…" With that, Ben sat in the waiting area and picked up a football magazine to read.

He watched over the magazine as Connie called Bob and had an agitated conversation. He smiled when she hung up and the office door behind her opened.

"Ben! Good to see you!" Bob bellowed from his office door.

Ben put down the magazine and walked slowly into Bob's office, exchanging handshakes and smiles as Bob ushered him in.

"You had no need to fly all the way here," Bob said as he offered Ben a seat. "We were about to call you."

Ben doubted that very much. "I have some important business to attend to at HQ and possibly a trip to Tampa Bay."

Bob eyed Ben, evidently deciding to ignore the Tampa reference for now.

"Let's get to it, Ben. Time is money. We want 51% of the Cougars: take or leave it."

"And in return?"

"A small percent of stock for you in the Texan organization."

"Really?" Ben tried to read Bob's face, like a poker player at Las Vegas. "How have you calculated the value of my small amount of stock in the Texans?"

"The value of the Cougars and Texans as it stands today. There is a vast difference between the two, Ben."

"Interesting! I have Tampa Bay offering me a sweeter deal," he lied. "The investment I have made in the Cougars will come to fruition over five years. That is in my plan, which you've no doubt studied. I will meet you in the middle with the value projected over three years. With that done, we should cover my contract."

"Contract? You will have a seat on our board, be a proud member of the NFL – your dream, Ben."

"My contract will allow me to continue running the Cougars, along with having a say in the operations of the Texans. The GM will report to me; I will be involved in the signing and release of players."

Bob narrowed his eyes, "You don't have enough football knowledge, no track record."

"The Cougars are doing fine."

"That's the UK, Ben."

"The game is universal, regardless of location."

"What other strange requests do you have before I go back to the board?"

"I want the Texans to give Harry Smith a try-out."

"You see?" Bob smacked the desk and made to stand up. "Precisely what I was just saying. No football knowledge. That's a ridiculous proposition."

"Why? Because he's British? He played at UT. Won them the bowl! What is your problem? It would be fantastic PR for the team. He probably won't make the cut but it would show the Texans are cutting-edge, open to trying a fresh approach."

Bob laughed. "We just won the Super Bowl! Isn't that fresh enough for you?"

"Yeah, sure, but it took you fifteen years to do it. Let me ask you this: after last year's college season, if Harry had been eligible to be drafted, where would you have taken him?"

"I am not the GM or part of the draft process."

"Just saying. You've been around the game long enough. Give it a stab."

"Ninth round."

"Okay. I would have said sixth after the Cotton Bowl. Tom Brady was taken in the sixth. Okay, ninth. Let me see. Johnny Unitas, Kurt Warner and Romo never even made the draft."

"Harry is also a bit small for a QB, don't you agree?"

"Look at QBs like Wilson at Seattle. And the legendary Flutie is an inch shorter than Harry. Receivers like Largent and Welker are totally undersized."

"I see you know your NFL history."

"You bet."

Bob thought hard.

"Look, let's wait on the outcome of your counter offer. I'll call you first thing in the morning. If we have a deal, you can drop by to sign the papers before flying back to jolly old England."

"Harry Smith?"

"Let's make a compromise on that one."

They shook hands.

Chapter 59

"Amy, I need you now," Harry said in a sexy actor's voice.

"What's up, you bonehead?"

"I am the guy to take the Cougars all the way to win the championship and I can't get it out of my head. Its driving me crazy and the solution is some quality Amy-time."

"Well, aren't you the psychic one? I was just about to call you with some news."

"Tell me. Make it good."

"Alright. Calm down, will you? I have a cabin in a spa resort. A friend of my dad's asked if I would write a short blurb for their website and take a few photographs. In return, I get two nights free in the Cotswolds."

"Sounds brilliant. When are you thinking?"

"Now. I'll pick you up in forty-five minutes."

"No way! I can't do that! I have special training this afternoon and a new playbook to start studying for the big game."

"Are you saying no to a wild weekend with your girl?"

"Heck no, it's exactly what I need. Tell you what. Send me the postal code and cabin number. I'll put it in my satnav and be there tonight. I promise."

"Fair enough. Don't be late."

Harry finished practice, packed his playbook in an

overnight bag, and with the exception of one stop on the way, he was all Amy's.

Harry found Brad in the orthopedic ward, his leg fully bandaged with a large pin inserted in his knee. When Harry poked his head in the door, Brad glowered.

"Harry Smith. Here to gloat?"

"No I'm not here to gloat, you ass. I just found out you're going back to Oregon, gone for the season. I had to say bye."

Brad's face softened. "Harry, what I said about Amy was shit. We all knew at training camp she only had eyes for you. She's gorgeous, you lucky bastard."

"I know."

"Beat the Ravens for me Harry – for the team and the city of Leeds. I'll miss you all. Show them why you were the first Brit to play in my country. It's our game, not yours – I don't know how you did it. Man, I was throwing a football when I was three."

"Thing is, Brad, I was on an amazing team where the read option was perfect. I love watching you play. You are so relaxed in the pocket. What I wouldn't give for your throwing action."

"Well, the Ravens will have two spies on you, so when you can, think about what I would do. Try staying in the pocket a bit more."

"Will do. Take care of yourself, Brad."

They shook hands.

"Keep in touch, okay?"

Chapter 60

Amy soaked in the hot tub, totally naked, drinking a glass of Moet Chandon.

Above her the big sky glimmered with stars beginning to twinkle in all directions. She took a deep breath, taking in the dusk emerging and the sun disappearing behind the last speck of pink sky on the horizon.

"Harry, where are you?" she called. "I have a glass of champagne here for you that is losing its fizz."

He'd only just arrived an hour ago which pissed her off to no end. She'd already decided it was time to reveal her true feelings for him, tonight, without any talk of her career as the Cougar girl. Hopefully she could have both, but she wanted Harry and had hated their cool-off period. *Your idea, girl.*

Harry appeared, wearing a pair of boxers, and slipped into the tub on her other side.

"You do realize I am starkers in here while you have those silly boxer shorts on? Sometimes you are a total numpty." Harry smiled, not looking Amy in the eyes.

"Okay, Harry. Let's put all our cards on the table. You seemed to be a tad jealous of my friendship with Ben Shannon, and probably thought that was the reason for the cool-off. It wasn't. I was given the best opportunity thus far in my short career and I took it. But I couldn't do my job properly if I was all wrapped up in you. I do think the world of Ben Shannon and respect him immensely. I believe the three of us are an amazing team and together we've come this far with the Cougars and will win the bowl game. End of story, as far as Ben is concerned. I want this relationship to move to the next level, but I need for you to trust me."

"I do and …" He still wouldn't meet her eyes.

"What? Spit it out, Harry." She was starting to worry.

"I've kept a secret from you about Ben. I've wanted to tell you for weeks, but Ben swore me to secrecy. He is a very private man."

He told Amy everything about his wife losing their daughter and how he imagined she would have grown up to be like Amy.

Harry came closer, his arm slipping around Amy's shoulders. Suddenly she couldn't stand to be touched. She removed his arm, moving to the other side of the tub. "Why did neither one of you confide in me? I just said we're a great team and now this piece of news? Men!"

"It was a pure coincidence. Timing is everything. I caught him with his guard down, drunk and upset. Out of all the days of the year, I happened to pick that day."

"Why did you go round there in the first place?"

Harry made a face in answer. Amy studied him, puzzled, until she finally realized.

"What? You actually went to him with that nonsense about me and him?"

"Sorry Amy, I really mean it. It was stupid. I understood that as soon as I got there."

"That midnight phone call – when you said you were doing all that thinking – it was all a total lie!"

"Not really. After I got back from his house, I did a lot of thinking. Maybe I told you a white lie but my feelings for you were – are – off the charts. Plus, I was still in shock from talking to Ben, seeing him in such a state. We seemed to bond that night. He made me give my word I would keep it in confidence, even from you!"

She wanted to forgive him. She wanted to accept that, but what he'd done was too much. She stared at the bubbling water in stony silence.

"I guess leaving my shorts on would be a good idea." He grinned, obviously trying to soften the mood.

"Actually, the tub has gone really cold all of a sudden." She got out, cascading water all over him, and wrapped up tightly in her towel.

Harry had the sense not to follow, to give her some space. She took a long cool shower, slowly increasing the heat until it was piping hot. She thought hard on the conversation with Harry – Ben's strong bond with her now making complete sense. *I have to forgive both of them. Part of this was my fault.* But she couldn't face Harry quite yet.

Without meaning to, she imagined Harry in the shower with her, massaging her back, his body pressed hard against her ass, his fingers kneading gently into her shoulders. Finally she relaxed – not just that, but got bloody horny. She loved him, wanted him so bad.

I'll forgive him, right now. She wrapped a short towel around her body, listening to the muffled sound of music from the living room. She pulled on her tight t-shirt off the bed and opened the door to the living room. The music resonated throughout the room.

"U2? What an old fart you are," she exclaimed.

"I often listen to them when the mood takes me. Come here and dance with me."

They danced, Harry swirling her around in some type of slow jive. He pushed his hand hard against hers, releasing her to fall on the sofa. Harry turned the music down just a smidgen and began singing. *You're the real thing, the real thing, even better than the real thing, child.* The guitar solo came on and Harry played along, air guitar style.

"What are you doing?" she said giggling.

It's Edge, the man himself."

"Turn the music down and talk to me. I keep learning more about your quirks. U2 fanatic at 23? Get hip, will you?"

"Now there's a story." He smiled. "Paul – my G Pops – has another story besides football. He was a New Romantic, but really he loved U2. Back in the late seventies he saw them at some university concert, and has followed them ever since. Anyway, he passed on his passion for U2 to my dad and down to me – three generations."

"Brilliant story. Now I get why you like them so much."

"Yeah. Hey, not to change the subject, but the fact that you're wearing no bottoms is turning me on like crazy. I have an idea. Why don't you perform your famous lap dance, like our first night?"

She hit him hard on the shoulder, slowly rising to her feet, dancing, moving her hips seductively. His eyes were glued to her, fever bright.

"Funny, I quite like U2 after all."

Bono's voice reached the chorus of the song, *She moves in mysterious ways.*

"Yes she does, and don't you forget it, buddy."

Chapter 61

"Good morning, Connie. How are you this morning?" Ben was in fine form today. He had a spring in his step that had been missing for quite some time.

"I'm just peachy, Mr. Shannon. I'm afraid Bob is running thirty minutes late. May I get you a coffee?"

All above board, even after last night. The consummate professional. He smiled.

"Yes, please. Cream, no sugar.

Ben watched her get the coffee, admiring her. *I'll be back in a few months. Maybe this time I could try to hold down a relationship, leave the past behind me.*

"Your coffee, Mr. Shannon." She left without another word, back behind her desk, cool as could be. The only clue that something was different was the flash of her eyes. Last night had been a different matter.

He had come out of the meeting with Bob, stalling in reception with the excuse of answering a text message. Bob had returned to his office. He'd put away his phone, moved to Connie's desk and blurted out, "How about dinner tonight?"

She'd said yes, and they had arranged to meet at Christies, the famous steakhouse in Houston. They'd had a blast, learning they had many hobbies in common. She loved good wine, played golf at a 7 handicap and watched most sports – including football. What a catch! Divorced, with no inkling to settle down again. Totally loved her job with the Texans.

It was her idea to continue the evening with some country dancing. As a student, he'd often frequented kicker bars. Fortunately, he'd transcended to a higher class of establishment and with a quick cab ride they were ordering drinks and watching the dancers.

Basically the room was a round house, a dance floor in a circle. That's what he usually told friends from England. He always made a point of taking his buddies to C & W bars just to watch their faces.

Ben had learned the dance within the first three months of landing in Houston, back in '89. It paid huge dividends for picking up gorgeous Texan women. He actually devised a trick whereby he would ask for a dance with a strong British accent. That alone was usually enough to be invited back for coffee. Once on the dance floor, he would ask for instructions on how to dance the two-step.

"This is my first time in Texas," he'd purr. "I just landed this afternoon. I have an important meeting in the morning – oil business."

By the end of the dance, he would be complimenting his partner, "You are such a good teacher. I thought it would take me forever to learn that dance."

"Just keep talking, honey, and I will teach you anything your heart desires," they would always offer with their sweet Texan drawl.

Last night with Connie, there'd been no need for any

tricks on the dance floor. They moved around like they had been lifelong dance partners. They moved as one.

He had decided to offer her coffee at his place – back to his big house in River Oaks where he never invited ladies. Never since his wife had gone. Last night he'd told himself to step up, leave the past in the past.

He had half expected she would ask for a guided tour. He would show her the whole house, and his wine collection. Funny thing about dancing as partners is all about connection. The two-step might not be the prettiest – certainly not sultry like the Tango – but man, that feeling of connection, physically, mentally.

They had both felt it, and once alone in private the urge to rip each other's clothes off was so strong. They'd made passionate love, right there in the living room. He recalled hoping the housekeeper was hard asleep. Funny, the next morning, breakfast was served in bed for two.

"Ben, sorry to keep you waiting. Please come in," Bob interrupted his thoughts of last night's experience.

"Okay, Ben, we have a deal. The board has agreed you will have a slightly bigger stake in the Texans with involvement in operations. We do expect to see a great return on the Cougars. We will continue to apply pressure on the NFL to ensure we make the whole European plan a huge success."

Ben signed the documents, trying to keep a big grin from appearing on his face. "Please don't release this to the press for twenty-four hours."

"No problem."

On the way out he said goodbye to Connie, making sure they were alone.

"I'll be back next month. Could I see you again?"

"We're about to announce your position with the Houston Texans, Mr. Shannon. I heard through the grapevine you don't mix business with pleasure."

"We could be discreet."

She quickly stroked his hand, glancing in all directions. "You have a date."

Chapter 62

Amy joined Harry in the shower. She always had a one-track mind in the morning.

"Need my coffee, Amy. I'm half asleep." He was probably coming across as a Neanderthal, judging by her laughing smile.

"Shut up," she said, insisting on her ideas of what a shower was for.

Morning person or not, he wasn't putting up a fight. Afterward, she slipped out of the shower with a smile and left him to wake up on his own. He stood under the hot water until he came alive, then he shut off the water and toweled off.

"Is the coffee brewed?" he called.

"Yes, of course. Dark roast from Columbia. Pancakes, too."

Harry devoured the coffee, his hands tightly around the mug. "Smells good."

They ate pancakes, drank lots of coffee. Harry was in heaven and pumped for the game. The only thing better was having Amy back in his life for good. He gazed at her across the table.

"Have you spoken with Kelly lately?" she asked.

"Whoa, where the heck did that come from?" Harry felt like the ground had suddenly opened up beneath him.

"Have you ever heard of female intuition?"

"Oh yeah. My mum is a master of that particular talent."

"Well, we are together right? No more cooling off. We've revealed our secrets, promised never to hide anything again. So, answer my question."

Despite the warning bells going off in his head, he answered, "Yes, I have. I have so many friends in Austin – hell, the state of Texas. Kelly knows most of them. It wasn't right to ignore her. She asked if she should visit me in Leeds, if there would be any way to save our relationship. I said no, but I had to use the old cliché 'let's stay friends'. You'll find her on my Facebook friends list. It wasn't fair to her or my friends. Kelly did nothing wrong. It was the accident that changed me."

He held his breath, waiting for the explosion, but to his relief, none came.

"So we are okay, right? I mean this time next week we'll be in the Caribbean for two weeks, just the two of us with no distractions. Kelly won't be a distraction, right?"

"No, she won't. I can't wait." He squeezed her hand tightly. "I do have one more secret. Kind of a surprise, really. It's funny you should mention speaking with Kelly and my friends at UT. When I was in the doldrums last year, I called my professor. I studied my final year online with video conferencing, taking my final exams under the watchful eye of his colleague at Bristol University."

"Bloody hell! And you passed?"

"Of course I did. I now have an MBA in Finance."

"Who knows about this?"

"Just my Mum and Dad."

"You haven't told Paul?"

"No. I was waiting for the right moment."

"What about your graduation? You missed it."

"All will be revealed when we see my G Pops, together."

"Well make it quick, will you?"

"Yep, I will. And, Amy, you understand that Kelly and I are officially just friends, right? That's not going to change."

"I believe you. Nice surprise, though. You do seem to surprise me often, which is a good thing. I only have one more thing to say to you, Harry Smith, and this needs to be said. The game on Sunday – you're the starting QB. The Cougars' dreams are resting on your shoulders."

He tried to move his hand, but she kept a hold of him like a vice grip. "I know the accident changed you on the field. I totally understand. I'm different after the attack, too. I never said anything at the time, but according to the doctor I technically died before you saved me on that horrible day. I've had weird dreams – I changed too. That was partly why I needed space from you. My feelings were so strong for you, like we were fated to be together. That was way too quick for us. I didn't want to scare you off."

Harry now squeezed her hand tightly.

"What a ninny! You could never put me off. Do you realize I've been feeling the same way? You've inspired my whole comeback. You made me realize I need to show the UK – our fans – just how good I was in Texas. I won't be the same Harry as back then. I'll be better."

"Now that is the Harry Smith we all love."

"So that includes you with the love thing, right?"

"Maybe." She looked at him coyly, and his heart filled with hope.

Chapter 63

Amy received two urgent text messages from Ben. *Please come to dinner at my place tonight, 6.00 sharp. It's compulsory.* He finished it off with a smiley face.

She looked at all the recipients. Harry and Paul! *Gosh, are we all becoming a family? 6.00 is really early for dinner.*

The second was a question – *What is your deadline time for a story?* She called Geoff at the *Gazette*.

"Amy! So nice to hear from you. We don't get to speak with each other too often. What can I do for you?" Geoff seemed to have a crush on Amy and went out of his way to help her when it came down to the wire. She felt bad for exploiting him, but in a pinch …

"What is the latest time I can have a story to you this evening? It'll be front page in the sports section."

"That's big. It would require some shifting around. Is the boss cool with it?"

"He will be, I promise."

"10:00PM."

"You're a sweetheart. Look out for it."

"Hey, are you still seeing Harry Smith? It's just that I was going to ask you out to that new wine bar."

"Sorry, still seeing him. Tell you what though, I'll drop you off a really nice wine in the morning."

"Okay," he sighed.

Chapter 64

Ben had hired a chef, but he preferred to look after the expensive wines personally and match them perfectly to each course. They spoke about a variety of topics until after dessert. Finally Ben stood up, pacing around the room like a cat on a hot tin roof.

"What is it?" asked Harry.

"Okay, here we go. Amy, you may wish to take notes so you can make that deadline. First, let us all raise our glasses to the Cougars – a fine first season regardless of the bowl outcome this Sunday. Cheers."

"What do you mean regardless of Sunday? We are going to win," Harry said confidently.

"I have a lot to say, and I want to start by saying you've given me one of the best years of my life.

"Hear, hear," Paul shouted.

"I'd been so absorbed in my work, the thrill hadn't been the same. The Cougars and the three of you have changed my outlook on life. As you know, my dream was to be part of an NFL team. It's well documented." He laughed. "I flew straight back today from the US with news that will change the level of American football in the UK. I expect it to become a top three sport in the country – not tomorrow or next year, but inevitably and soon.

"I've fulfilled my dream to be involved with the NFL.

Not an outright owner, but a shareholder."

The room went into silence. Amy glanced at Harry in disbelief.

"What about the future of the Cougars?" Harry asked.

"Stop keeping us in suspense, Ben," Amy pleaded.

"It's all about the Cougars. The future is only bright. Thing is, while I will come back for the Cougar season, Amy, I would like you and Harry to go to the USA. I imagine Paul would be delighted to get back home to Texas."

They all looked again at Ben, totally stunned. But Ben wasn't finished.

"I am now a shareholder in the Houston Texans with some clout in the running of the team." He looked significantly at Harry.

"Super Bowl champs? You are kidding, right?" Harry sounded totally dumbfounded.

"So, let me get this straight." Amy held Harry's hand tightly on the table. "We're all invited to work for the Texans?"

"You bet."

"But how? What, Harry?" stammered Amy.

"I need a right-hand assistant, working mainly in the PR department and marketing. Website development, social networking – all right up your alley, Amy."

"Harry gets to try-out next year at training camp?" Paul asked.

"What if he doesn't make it?"

"Think positive, Amy." Ben took a sip of his wine. "You usually do."

"Well, this is my cue," said Harry, looking as proud as a

peacock. "I graduated from UT with an MBA in Finance. I received a text today that they've arranged a special graduation party for me, since I was busy playing for the Cougars in May. My professor will be doing the ceremony with all my friends in attendance. After that, we'll have a big party on the lake in North Austin – live music and barbeque, Texas style."

Paul clapped him on the back with overjoyed congratulations. Ben added his own.

"You see, I always have options. I can try out with the Texans with absolutely no pressure. If I don't make it, which is likely – Amy's right – Ben can still offer me a high paid top position with one of his companies. Anyway, in the meantime, I would like to officially invite all three of you to my graduation party."

Ben and Amy laughed.

"Try keeping us away," Amy said.

Paul excused himself, tears in his eyes, "I need a breath of fresh air." Amy watched him go, dismayed. Harry put a hand on her shoulder and rose.

"I'll go have a drink with him on the patio. G Pops will be bawling if I leave him alone. He could not have wished for better news than this. By the way, Ben, I had to tell her our secret. I kept it from her for far too long." He headed for the patio door.

"Aw shit." Ben looked down, left alone with Amy at the table. His eyes stung with tears.

"Ben, its fine. I should have realized it was something like that. I often feel the same. I have a wonderful dad and yet there is always room for one more. You've been like a father to me." She reached for his hand across the table and smiled at him. "Hey, I have a question about the Texan deal."

"Shoot."

"Are you offering me a job due to our friendship, your paternal feelings or just needing to have your adopted daughter close by? I mean, holy crap, I am only 24!"

"Amy, let's just say I had a daughter and a happy marriage: it would not change how I feel about you. I would have met you that day in Bradford and immediately taken a shine to you. I saw great potential and you've proved my instincts were bang on. You're a smashing young lady and I want you on our team in Texas."

Amy went to him, "Hey, big guy, I need a hug." She held him tight for a moment.

"Right. Let's fill our glasses and see how Paul is doing. He was so overcome with emotion with all that news."

"Maybe I could do with a little cry myself," said Amy quietly.

Chapter 65

A sell-out crowd of 84,000 for the bowl game at Wembley had been announced earlier in the day. Harry read the four-page story on the NFL announcement earlier in the week with debates and opinions from analyst and experts. Football had moved to #5 on the top watched sports. It was a leap from #8, only five years ago. British fans couldn't get enough, and yet they wanted more – something more British, their own identity. The Brits usually loved Americans, but hated them more than anyone else in a sporting competition.

The writers were comparing it to the Ryder Cup in golf. You can only watch the PGA and the four majors for so long. Patience ran thin between Brits and Americans alike: being nice, congratulating each other, *fine shot there*. The Ryder Cup changed all that. For one week, Americans and Brits hated each other.

The enmity only increased when it came to Europe and this was one of the debates. Some called for resurrecting the NFL Europe League. It wasn't logistically possible to have NFL teams based in the UK for the entire season. But they had calculated that teams such as New York, Baltimore, and basically all on the eastern seaboard could be in the UK almost as quick as flying to Los Angeles or San Francisco. It had come as a surprise, with that in mind, that Houston was one of the first two teams. Credit was going to the visionary skills of the Houston Texan organization and Ben Shannon of the Leeds Cougars.

Nice one, Ben, Harry thought.

So far, the New York Giants and The Houston Texans would each play all four preseason games in the UK. The Cougar Dome would play host to all the Texan preseason games along with two additional NFL games. The Texans would commit to one game in late October, playing the Patriots.

Harry paused reading at that point. That would be a great game, but difficult to watch without Tom Brady, who would have just retired. Over the next three years, the NFL big shots would analyze and plan out their strategy. The Giants and Texans expansion franchise mergers were a good start.

It had come as a big surprise that the Cowboys had not bought into the London Ravens. The paper cited that owner Denis Bazan made a sudden deal with New York, under the radar. Everyone agreed it was out of character for him.

Harry stared out of the bus window. Lines of fans wearing their Cougar blue and gold mingled with the black and gold of the Ravens, along with many other NFL team colours.

Harry couldn't believe it. Now this was more like the Longhorns. He leaned out the window and shouted, "Yee haw!"

The other players were just as revved up – one running to the toilet, others looking green. Big match-day jitters were hard to overcome.

Harry was ready for this game like no other before. His

phone chimed with a text from Amy wishing him the best, with pictures attached of homes outside of the city of Houston. She didn't waste any time. She had calculated pound to dollar conversion and the price attached to these mansions was an astonishingly low amount to basically be living like the lord of the manor.

He read the text with a smile. *You bet*, he replied.

That weekend had made him realize all of his problems since the accident were really quite simple. *I lost my love for the game, the will to win. Hell, I almost became a Buddhist, more interested in saving a wasp from being swatted. I don't know what my problem was or how I solved it. One thing I do know: I love Amy, I will make her proud today, and it's off back to Texas.*

Chapter 66

The first half was drawing to a close with the Cougars yet to score. Ravens had scored on their opening drive with the game becoming a defensive stalemate thereafter.

At the two-minute warning, Harry went to the sidelines to discuss the last series of plays before the half-time whistle.

"We have to do something different, coach!" he yelled. "If I throw short passes on the first two plays, do you have something on third down that might fool them?"

"If they keep using the outside blitz I do," said Coach Greaves confidently.

"Texas style. I know what you have in mind," said Harry with a smile.

He threw short passes for only a marginal gain on the next two plays. The Ravens were employing an aggressive outside blitz scheme.

This is going according to plan. Football was like playing chess on a large field. Sometimes plays were not designed to guarantee immediate success. They were moves designed to set up the defense for the big play to come later. *Come on coach give me the word. It will be Déjà vu, Longhorn style.*

Third and eight with the clock ticking down, Harry was in the huddle. "Do it," came the voice of Coach Greaves through his helmet.

"Spread formation, Texas hold 'em, on two," whispered Harry in the huddle. The players smiled. The slot receivers and the tight end joined the wide outs. The Ravens would suspect a pass and continue in their attacking mode.

"Hut hut!" Harry dropped back. The defenders charged, heading for him, at speed from both ends. He faked a pass to the right, tucked in the ball and ran straight through the middle untouched.

Touchdown!

The whistle blew for half-time. The Cougars players ran off the field, each player finding Harry for a congratulatory high five. Suddenly a Ravens linebacker sideswiped him, and he almost fell to the ground.

"You're going down in the second half!" came a gruff New York voice. "I'll knock your head off, you fucking Tex-Ass hand-me-down. Nobody tricks my defense."

The Cougar players all turned, ready to protect their QB, but the Ravens player had already sprinted to the other side of the field, his middle finger pointing to the sky.

"Fucking dirty Ravens," the Cougar players shouted simultaneously.

I am doing my best, he thought at the end of the third quarter. *Just wish I could throw a long ball.*

With less than two minutes to the whistle, the Ravens were winning by three points, 16-13.

The Ravens had managed two field goals to one field goal by the Cougars.

Harry called the huddle. They were second and 10 on the halfway line.

I could try for better field position and hope Billy can kick a field goal to tie the game. Shit, I hate the idea of extra time. Harry mulled over the problem in his mind.

Will they go into a 'prevent' defense, with the safeties playing deep or continue to attack? Stop over-analysing, mate, go for it all on this play, he concluded. Harry shouted the play and took three steps back. BOOM! Out of nowhere, the Ravens' defensive end hit him hard under the chin on a blitz play.

Harry was back in space – right back in the same spot he'd visited so many times after his accident.

The spiral arm of stars glistened. The soft voices seemed louder than before. The pull to the black abyss was stronger this time, taking all his might to keep from being pulled away. He looked hard at the stars.

It seems there could be faces, millions of them moving in between.

A shooting star, moving quickly, whistled by him, heading for the darkness.

The black force grew stronger. He pushed hard to stay in place. A small number of stars broke from the spiral arm, forming a shape he recognized. It was a horoscope symbol he knew. His mum had books and often offered to work on birth charts for friends and family. The stars stayed in that position for a few minutes, still moving in closer. Twelve stars – the same number on his jersey and Tom Brady's. They finally came to rest, close now, in two rows of six. A jury?

"You are not judging me. You can't decide my fate, my destiny. Not today!" he yelled.

Images in his mind suddenly seemed to transport in front of him, like a hologram. He blinked his eyes. The images were so vivid, like the millions of stars dancing in all directions. Every small detail was magnified with such perfect clarity, his brain now razor sharp.

He was driving in a flash car, a Ferrari with the top down. It was a long road with the hot sun beating down, not another car in sight. It had to be Texas. Amy was in the passenger seat, her long dark hair flowing in the wind, her left arm draped over his shoulder.

"Wow," he whispered. Her hand, the third finger, displayed a diamond ring, accompanied by a white gold band.

The next image was of him. He was in full football uniform, preparing to throw the ball. Again, the image was so vivid he could clearly see his hand holding the football in a most peculiar fashion.

"What the heck am I doing?" he muttered. On further investigation he realized the hand was at the back of the ball, with his index finger on the point of the ball rather than on the laces like most QBs. In fact, there was really only one famous player to throw in this style. Terry Bradshaw. He was the only one besides Brady and Montana to win four Super Bowls.

"I would never throw that way. I fucking tried it years ago. Now get me back, you lot!" He shouted in the general direction of the stars.

"Hey, I know what is going on here. It all seems clear to me this time. I'm not coming to you or going over there." He pointed to the darkness. "I know my destiny and I will fulfill it – you just watch me! Amy, Texas, the first British player to play QB in the NFL. Send me back right now!"

Chapter 67

In the stands, Amy was biting her fingernails. Paul was fidgeting on his seat. Ben had insisted they sit in the Cougar private box rather than with the press. After all, they would all be in Texas next month – Amy working with the Texans.

"Guys," Ben said, looking pale, "I left out one tiny detail with the Texan deal. You know what a stretch it would be for Harry to make the team. I had to plead with them just to get him into training camp."

"I know," they both said in unison.

"The actual deal was he had to play a blinder today and lead the Cougars to a win."

"Ben, I want to throttle you…" The roar of the crowd drowned out Amy's final words. Harry was on his feet.

Chapter 68

Big Mike the offense guard pulled Harry up from the ground. "What was that Harry? Send me back where?"
"Never mind, let's win this game."
"Not so fast, Harry Smith," said the ref. "What is your name?"
"Errm Harry Smith."
"Where are you?"
"At Wembley, playing in the bowl game."
"How many fingers?" He held up his hand.
"Three."
"Okay, you may continue." The ref jogged out of the way.

The coaches had taken their final time out. Messages came through his helmet: "How are you Harry?" "Okay your next play is …" He shut himself off from the sound – no coaches barking out instructions. He was totally focused.

"Huddle up!" he shouted to the players. "Okay, this is all on Isolation."

"Me?" said Leroy, the quick wide receiver.

"Yes, you."

Leroy had been starved this year with the Cougars. The offense style did not call for a fast wide receiver that went down field and had good hands. He had written a rap song entitled 'Isolation' in honour of being totally pissed off about never getting the ball.

"We have time for two more plays and the Ravens know I can only throw 20 yards. We will only need this one play. Leroy, you'll run a 20-yard hook/out, Phoenix 55. You know that play?"

"Course I know, cuz. Just haven't seen it come to me this year."

"Okay. When you break for the sideline, make it look good. Get the corner to bite, then change your pattern to a fly. This is the big play. All of you play it exactly as a 55, except Leroy. Break."

Under the huddle, Harry shouted three times Phoenix 55. The Ravens defense players were smiling as if to say "Yeah, let him have his 20 yards."

"Hut hut!" shouted Harry.

Harry stepped back four, maybe five times, watching the play develop. Leroy made a perfect cut and fake, the cornerback was sold on the play, the free safety was playing up guessing on a shorter pass. He must have been 70 yards from the end zone, he figured.

He threw the ball hard; rotating so fast it looked like a torpedo piercing through the water. The ball was on course for the end zone, the tip of the ball straight. It started to arc down around the 10-yard line. Leroy caught the ball, on his tiptoes, dangerously close to the sideline.

Great hands Leroy, now just stay in bounds.

He looked at the side umpire – all seemed good.

Leroy made it to the end zone. The Cougar players surrounded him while he imitated an old Usher dance routine. Harry held his breath.

Is it a TD? Have we won the bowl?

Harry instinctively looked to the Cougars fans, some 40,000 strong. They roared loud. He checked the giant screens. *TD* flashed, followed by the message: *Leeds Cougars, the new UK bowl champions.*

The players lifted him on their shoulders. The giant screen flashed a new message: *Harry Smith MVP*.

"Guys, give me a minute," Harry shouted, jumping off the head of one of the huge linemen. He caught sight of Amy and ran across the field to the sideline.

"I can't believe it," he shouted while he picked her off her feet, spinning her around. Paul was trying to hug them both.

"Put me down right now! You had us scared there for a minute! You were out for the count," Amy shouted, and laughed and teared up all in one moment.

"I made a quick visit to a familiar place, but this time I wanted to get right back here and win the game."

"What? You're making no sense!" Amy laughed.

"Never mind. It's a long story. I'll tell you when we get to Texas."

Amy ran back into his arms. "I love you, Harry Smith."

"I love you, too. More than anything."

"Hey Harry, it's time for the presentation," shouted one of the Cougar players. Harry was about to run, hesitated, spun around.

"Hey, G Pops!" he shouted above the noise around the stadium. Paul was dancing around singing, "I'm going to Texas!" Paul stopped, looked at Harry and grinned as wide as a Cheshire cat.

"I finally did it, G Pops."

Paul continued to smile, tears now in his eyes. "You looked just like Tom Brady with that pass."

"It was Bradshaw."

"Bradshaw?" Paul's tears now turned into laughter. "Hey, Brady and Harry wear the #12 jersey, and so did Bradshaw!"

"What did you do?" shouted Amy.

"I threw a long – perfect – tight spiral!"

A True Short Story

Chapter 1

Cotswold Bears 1987

It was a cold Sunday in Cheltenham Spa and I was under the bed covers reading the Sunday papers. I had a flat in a gorgeous Victorian house, almost in the centre of this fine Regency town in an area named Montpellier, with more wine bars than pubs. It was posh and home to the best private girls' school in the country. I loved staying in bed on cold Sunday mornings, reading my favorite newspapers with a big mug of strong coffee.

It was about 10.30 on this particular morning when I decided to read the local paper and prolong getting out of bed. I glanced through it, not seeing anything to catch my attention, as usual, until I came to the ads.

"The Cotswold Bears American football team is looking for new staff for the 1987 season. Practice begins at 2:00PM on Sunday.

"What the fuck?" I shouted. "That is today!"

The paper came out on a Thursday and I never looked at it until Sunday, if at all. I read it again. It did say staff and not just players. I would be an amazing coach! I knew the game. I had studied ever since the 1985 Super Bowl. I watched the 1986 game where the Chicago Bears demolished the Patriots with the famous 46 defense. I actually went all the way into

London to find a book on the game.

I have always been different and back then I had just moved from being a New Romantic in the late seventies when my friends had given up on me. After all, it's hard to be taken seriously by your fellow man when you wear make-up, dangling earrings and clothes from an antique shop from the 1920s, particularly living in Northern England!

I enjoyed American football over any other sport, knowing full well in England that would make someone seem extremely odd. It was a combination of rugby and chess to me and I was totally fascinated with the game.

I showered and called my mate who I was supposed to meet for a few pints at lunch. "Tim, I can't make it today, something has come up. Hey, question: have you heard of a team called the Cotswold Bears?"

"Course I have, mate. They had a winning record in their first season last year. Seems they were a bit boring, running the ball all the time, and not many fans showed up for the games. Why do you ask?"

"I thought about going down and helping out."

"What?" He laughed. "Have you been drinking this time of the morning?"

"Yes. Probably stupid, but if you don't see me, I have gone to take a gander."

I arrived at the playing field just before 2:00PM to witness a large turnout, with guys of all sizes wearing football helmets and shoulder pads performing stretch exercises.

I saw two guys barking out instructions to a group of players with clipboards, whistles around their necks, and realized they must be the coaches. They were also yanks, no doubt about it, strutting round like sergeant majors. One was a short stocky black guy that reminded me of the boxer Smoking Joe Frazier. The other was wearing expensive Ray Ban sunglasses. His hair was slicked back like some actor out of Hollywood.

I was thinking what to say when Mr. Hollywood shouted, "Yo, are you here to practice for the team or stand there like a knucklehead?"

I gained confidence, deciding there was no way I would let this cocky yank show me up, "I am here to apply for a coaching position."

By this time Smoking Joe had joined in and stared at me for a full minute, while the other coach smiled. "I am the head coach of the Cotswold Bears and we are looking for players. Are you interested?"

"No," I replied, "I have a bad leg. I'm more interested in using my knowledge of football to help the team."

He immediately barked back, "This is football, son, not soccer," and walked away.

I stared at Hollywood. "The ad in the paper said staff and players."

"Maybe we could consider you for equipment manager."

"Yes," I said, all excited. "What would that entail?"

He smiled and cocked his head to one side. "Cleaning all the players' jock straps, for one."

He left me there feeling like a total jerk.

I went home totally pissed off and remembered my granddad always telling me to hate the yanks, love the Canadians. Back then, it was bred into us at an early age – from our dads and granddads that had been around for World

War Two – Americans were flash bastards with big mouths, taking all our girls with stockings and chocolates to entice them into bed, while our lads were over there fighting the Jerries.

I found my coaching book and sat to study more about this amazing game that had partially taken over my life. I looked at all the diagrams, the variations on offence plays.

Okay, I have a plan, I thought. *I'll present it at their next practice session next week.*

Chapter 2

A few days later, I was at the playing field after work. This was a shorter practice than Sunday, under the floodlights. I made my way to Smoking Joe and Hollywood with a more confident approach than last Sunday.

"Guys," I said, trying to sound more American. "Okay, give me a task – something that will convince you both I know this game. I want to be a coach for the Bears this season, so tell me what the fuck I need to do to prove myself. I know what the quarterback is saying in the huddle, a wide receiver's routes – I even know what a Wishbone offense is all about. Come on. How many Brits know shit like that?"

They both looked a bit shocked and the head coach thought for a moment before his precise reply.

"The Torbay Trojans are in our league, a good team we will play twice in the season. Go to their first preseason game on Sunday and give me a scouting report." And at that he walked off in the direction of the players.

Hollywood smiled. "Let's see what you've got, sucker." He left me standing there on my own again.

I prepared for the Sunday game and never once did it dawn on me I would be driving all the way to Torbay in Devon on my own money, on my sacred day off. I had a clipboard, camera, recorder, and a flask of coffee with whisky in it. It was fucking freezing that day.

Writing in my notebook, taking pictures whenever the Trojans were on offense, I got all sorts of funny looks. I actually got to like it – a journalist, a spy, the James Bond of American football. Nobody asked and I just politely went about my business with a smile on my face.

I got back at some ridiculous hour and the next night did up the scouting report, had the pictures processed and packed it all neatly in a folder marked Torbay Trojans vs. Whitney Wildcats Scouting Report.

I did emphasize in the report that I had no idea what their offense did, no idea of the final score. I simply focused on the defense: weak side, strong side, which players over-pursued, the secondary coverage, zone, blitz, stopping the run – I had the lot! My goal was to be an offense coach, which is all about reading the opponent's defense.

At the next training secession that week, I tried all through practice to get the coach's attention. In the end, I had to wait until he was in the car park.

"Coach, I have your scouting report."

He turned to me and said, "Son, what the fuck are you talking about?" and at that he got in his car. He had obviously forgotten our conversation and my given task.

I tapped on the car door. The driver's window rolled down slowly. I tossed the report past his head to land on the passenger seat. Then I looked at him square in the eyes.

"Fuck off," I said with some conviction. I turned away, found my car. I needed a pint or four, fast.

I woke from heavy dreams to the sound of the phone. It was 11:45PM and I could not believe someone would call at this time of night. I picked up the phone.

"Coach here, have you got a second?"

"Errm what?" I groaned.

"You do know the game of American football. The scouting report was first-class and I liked how you spotted the right defensive end over pursues to the right. Report on Sunday to Coach JJ, our offense coach. You are our new assistant offense coach of the Cotswold Bears. Welcome aboard."

I fell back to sleep right away, proud I had stood up to them. I was on the coaching staff of our town's American football team, in the Budweiser league. All I had to do now was work under Hollywood!

Chapter 3

Our first preseason game was coming up fast, away to the Black Country Nailers – a name that conjured up horror movies to me. But apparently they were not so frightening, although they had a solid defense. This was merely a friendly game, a fine tune-up to prepare for the regular season which was looming fast, only a few weeks away.

We had been projected in both UK Gridiron Magazines to finish second in our division behind the mighty Plymouth Admirals. Plymouth was the champion of their division in 1986 with a 10-0 season.

Meanwhile, Hollywood and I had no chemistry, and I felt like a spare prick at a wedding. I had bought a video and book on coaching wide receivers that featured Steve Largent, the prolific wide receiver of the Seattle Seahawks. JJ had let me take the receivers for the last hour of practice and I was gaining their respect with some cutting-edge drills.

Most of practice time was conditioning in what the Americans called calisthenics. It sounded like a disease to me the first time they shouted to the players. I found the terminology somewhat bloody alien. The players reacted like it was disease and most did not look forward to this, especially the big linemen.

The midweek practice was usually fine; however, Sunday

mornings were a sight to behold. All the players had been out the night before and had a skin full, finishing off the night in the Cheltenham nightclub. Each of the big guys would take a turn running to the bushes to puke up, with no sympathy from either of the American coaches.

"Get back here now!" they would shout, with said player staggering back with sick sliding out of his mouth.

One lineman in particular was so funny. Turned out to be a great player, but in those early days he was there for a laugh and tried to wind up the Americans at every moment. He would wait for Hollywood to walk by while doing the squat jump exercise and let off the largest slimy fart you could imagine. Coach would shout obscenities at him and make him do extra laps at the end of practice.

We arrived at the ground in creepy Black Country, somewhere close to Wolverhampton, on a cold miserable March day. This area in the middle of England got its name from the soot during the heavy industrial days and when I saw their players dressed in black with very strange accents, I was ready for home. I was already shitting myself being at our first game and, while it was friendly, the anticipation of seeing our days of training and drills all come together, with players that were like friends to me about to get hit hard with full contact, was too much for me. I needed a drink!

The game is a distant memory. We won, and I think our defense had a clean sheet. The offense made many mistakes, the head coach called all the plays, and 95% were running plays. In effect, my receivers and I were not needed. I decided to make a bold move back on the bus. I sat next to Hollywood.

Before I could say a word, he looked at me and said, "Goddamnit, if Coach does not let me run the offense and call the plays, I'm outta here."

I agreed with him and added we would never win our division or even give Plymouth a game unless we started to pass the ball. "We have five passing plays in our playbook when the NFL has more than a hundred."

"Well this isn't the NFL and all our receivers are Brits. I will make a deal with you, I will ask for five more when I give him my demands. In return, I need you to commit more time to this team and to getting it better."

I nodded. We talked about life in general and ever since that bus ride home, he became a close friend.

Chapter 4

JJ got his way, which actually surprised me. Apparently, he had told the head coach to fuck off, that he was leaving the team. Fortunately word never reached the players after he only missed one training session. Coach had panicked, called him up to agree he should call the offense and I could have three more plays.

Most of the teams in our new division knew our reputation. Run the ball, solid defense, and if we did pass on a rare occasion, it would be short. I had added two short routes, mainly since our tight end was a new recruit, fresh from his earlier career as a professional goalkeeper in our British game of football – a local lad with incredible hands and perfect for the 10-yard slant passes.

My new trick was simply this. 1. Fly, which meant run like shit in a straight line and the quarterback would throw a long pass (only that would never happen in the old Bears days.) 2. Run 5 yards and break at 90 degrees towards the sideline. I made my first new play a 21. Run the 2 for 5 yards, fake the shoulder to make the defensive player commit and then carry on a fly.

We beat the Herford Chargers in a tight and defensive game. The chargers were tough with a full squad of Brits, who apparently worked at the SAS base close by. Say no more. What they lacked in American football skill, they made up for in toughness. We won 13-6 and were glad to get the season started in a winning way.

JJ asked me to spend the weekend at his place, on base, to watch videos and come up with an offense game plan.

We immediately improved on offense, winning four in a row on the road. Our first game at home was to be against the unbeaten Admirals. Plymouth was the absolute favorite to win the division, much like they had the previous season. We had a good crowd and certainly far more than we had seen at our away games. It was quite the stadium too, giving our fans a perfect view of the entire field.

I have no idea why, but neither I nor JJ had our A games that day, a problem which, by the way, would never be repeated. We played poorly, did not score a touchdown, and proved all the experts were correct and Plymouth would surely be crowned division champions.

We spent hours that following week going through game video, concluding we had been intimidated by Plymouth's reputation. We were totally in agreement that the same mistake would never occur again on our watch. However, we had now lost one game and they seemed unlikely to let a game slip away with all that talent.

We never looked back after that disappointment, winning the next four games by huge scores with our offense.

In June, I was actually in the paper for the first time, in an article describing JJ and I with the nickname The Blues Brothers: JJ with the Hollywood sunglasses, regardless of whether it was sunny or grey skies, and me with the look of Dan Ackroyd – or at least according to the players.

We beat Taunton 38-6 and Herford 51-6 after only

beating them by a TD the first game of the season, with a whopping 60-22 win over Torbay. A couple of bizarre events happened in that period which gave us the inspiration to play amazing football only a few months after that dreary day in the Black Country. I was mentioned in the paper each week with great comments from coaches and players on how I made the team more balanced with an excellent passing game.

CHAPTER 5

The Steve Grogan day made our British QB into a complete player. The New England Patriots superstar attended a special training day for our team. Due to fog at Heathrow airport, his plane was delayed. All the coaches had gone home except me. We had two QBs – one a Brit, one American. Kenny was from the good old US of A, while Kevin was from England. Kevin and I became good friends in 1987 and I was pleased he had waited for Grogan to arrive. After Grogan's education, Kev's first instinct was still to scramble. However, if and when it was required, he could now throw a ball 70 yards!

Mr. Grogan was a true gent and spent considerable time working our British QB with a drill on one knee, to give him an amazing throwing action. By the end, I had never seen Kevin throw the ball so long.

In the big win over Hereford that following week, I asked JJ for the 21 play. One of our receivers sprinted down the field. Kevin let loose, connecting for a 55-yard TD.

The other big news was thanks to the Hereford Chargers. They had beaten Plymouth in the shock result of our division. We were tied with the reigning champs with one loss as we headed into the final game of the season – Bears at Plymouth – to decide the divisional championship.

On game day, I woke up on the sofa with a blinding

headache. JJ and I had just spent two days and nights working on our plan, watching videos of Plymouth games over and over with special attention to our home game last month when they essentially kicked our butts.

We had finished each evening with our usual ritual of a game of darts accompanied by pints of Jim Beam and Coke. Darts was always about JJ beating a Brit at our treasured game – like we are all supposed to be brilliant at darts or cricket! He would always beat me on the final leg and I swear he had the board in his house rigged. Or maybe it was the bourbon. Living on a USA air force base had its perks, with bourbon being available at low cost, avoiding British taxes.

Chapter 6

JJ ran down the stairs, put on the coffee and started chatting, which was not my way of waking up in the morning.

"This is it Mikey, the big day."

No one ever called me Mikey but him.

I groaned, "Where is the coffee?"

He brought in a mug of coffee and continued in his upbeat manner, "This is what we have worked for all season."

"Can we pull off an upset? I mean, really?" I asked.

"I would not be spending all my fucking time on this if I didn't think we could win. Go get a shower. You look like shit."

We arrived at our ground to meet the players and make the journey down to Plymouth. I was amazed at the amount of fans to see us off and the extra buses for the fans, which numbered well above any previous away game. The cheerleaders' bus was packed full of fans and family members of the players.

Plymouth is a trek from Cheltenham and once we arrived at the ground, JJ and I were in need of a drink or two. Our tradition was always two pints of cider before a big game. We were not needed prior to the game or at half-time, since the head coach was brilliant with motivational stories and speeches to fire up the team. Also, we had taken over all the offense call plays and our defense coach was doing likewise, leaving our head coach to do what he did best.

Fifteen minutes to kickoff, we made our entrance on the sidelines to witness a crowd we had never seen at a Bears game. There seemed to be thousands rather than hundreds, and our relaxed composure from the cider quickly rose to a high octane level.

"Coach," he shouted to me, "get all the receivers and go through the game plan. The rest of the offense, with me, now."

We had two quarterbacks, a Brit and an American, but we had never used them as a true double weapon in a game. We started the American, who was a pocket quarterback with a good arm, while our Brit was a strong runner who could now throw a long ball after his day with legendary QB Steve Grogan. The theme was keeping them totally off balance.

Chapter 7

We started the game in dazzling fashion when Roy, one of our running backs, went straight up the middle for a 50+ yards TD. However, by half-time, we were down 14-12 in a tight physical game. Head coach was all over them, shouting at the players, "We can win this!"

JJ and I ran to the bar and downed a pint of cider at half-time.

"When are we going to start tricking them?" I asked impatiently.

He smiled. "Fourth quarter."

We legged it back. After the third quarter, the score was still too tight and we had only managed a field goal to go back in front by a point. One of our plays to introduce was a reverse. We had done this all season with success, except against Plymouth. They knew and expected we would try it.

This time, we had variations of the play. Reverse it, QB keep it, double reverse – you name it. When they stopped the reverse, the next play we faked and so on. In between, we would have either QB show reverse and then throw a long ball to our star wide receiver.

I had watched so many videos on the Admirals' defense, who were so disciplined and solid, but as we entered the fourth quarter they looked totally confused. We scored at will in the final quarter and went on to win 35-14.

I experienced some very proud moments that day – the fans singing, "We are number one, say we are number one." They may have only been a couple of hundred, but it looked and sounded like thousands to me.

The players got all the coaches on their heads and carried us to the crowd. I have been at huge games in the middle of singing fans, watching our team score, the atmosphere electrifying, but this was different – I was a member of the Cotswold Bears. The fans were singing, thanking us! I never imagined experiencing anything in sports that would have touched me so personally. We all have a standout year in our lives. 1987 would be in my top three.

I was so proud of a particular wide receiver that had an unbelievable day, with five catches for 129 yards and a record for any of our receivers. I asked him to try out for the Bears, knowing I would get some flack.

Before joining the team, he worked for me and we played tennis once per week. He was a fast bowler in cricket and a good athlete, however, he knew zero about the game of American football. The players said he was my favorite, which meant he had to prove himself more than the other players, week after week.

The most important part of this experience was that The Blues Brothers were champions and the respect and love we had for each other was unbreakable.

In the play-off game we were completely destroyed 66-0, and while that was unacceptable to the players, JJ and I didn't seem to care. We never truly got ready for that game, with our thoughts still on beating Plymouth. It took a great deal of energy from all of us, knowing full well without all the effort on any other given day, Plymouth would have won. That day was ours for our fans, the players and the coaches.

The following year, I moved to Texas.

★ ★ ★

Coach JJ La Torre, my close friend, suddenly passed away at the end of last year. He was only 49. He loved the game of football and played himself, in the running back position. However, what he loved the best was coaching Brits that had the passion but lacked the technique to play a new sport in England – American football. He made them all into players, part of something they could be proud of. He did the same with kids playing the game on the US base in England and later back in Connecticut. He made them winners, a life coach that helped turn them into fine young men. He managed to find time for all those kids while always being a great husband and father. His wonderful wife Jenny, his son Josh and his daughter Nicole were always the center of his attention.

The strangest thing, looking back at 1987 – our golden year coaching together – is he was only the ripe old age of 24.

A special man indeed, JJ, you are always in my thoughts and I know you are up there somewhere, coaching football.